Four Little Blossoms on Apple Tree Island

Mabel C. Hawley

FOUR LITTLE BLOSSOMS ON APPLE TREE ISLAND

BY

MABEL C. HAWLEY

AUTHOR OF "FOUR LITTLE BLOSSOMS AT BROOKSIDE FARM,
" "FOUR LITTLE BLOSSOMS AT OAK HILL SCHOOL, " ETC.

CONTENTS

CHAPTER I

THE NEW CAR

Half of a small boy protruded from the oven, his stout tan shoes waving convulsively.

"Twaddles! " Nora coming into her orderly kitchen was amazed. "Glory be, child, are you making toast of yourself? "

The shoes gave a final wriggle and Twaddles deftly backed out of the oven, turning to show a flushed face and a pair of dark, dancing eyes.

"What are ye doing? " insisted Norah curiously. "The sponge cake was baked and put away hours ago. "

"Oh, I don't want any of your sponge cake, " Twaddles assured her loftily, forgetting, perhaps, the many times he had hung around the kitchen door during Norah's baking and teased for "just one bite. " "I'm life-saving, Norah. "

"You're what? " asked Norah incredulously.

Twaddles sat down comfortably on the stone hearth before the old-fashioned coal range and began to clean caked mud from the soles of his shoes.

"It's a robin, " he explained. "A sick robin, Norah. I found him on the grass, and he was too cold and wet to fly. Mother used to put 'em in the oven when she was a little girl and that made 'em all well again. "

"You'll scorch him, " said Norah, stooping down to look. "That oven is nearly hot enough to bake biscuit in, Twaddles. Wait, I'll wrap your robin up in cotton and we'll put him on the shelf warmer; that's about the temperature he needs. "

Twaddles, assured of expert attention for his patient, scrambled to his feet.

1

"I have to go out in front and watch for Daddy, " he announced importantly. "I want to see what color the new car's painted. Sam said to be sure and write him. "

Norah, working over the faintly peeping young robin, blushed very red.

"You take the brush pan and broom, " she directed Twaddles, "and brush up that mud. Wasn't it only this morning your mother was telling you not to be making extra work? "

Twaddles obediently seized the dustpan and the long-handled broom. His intentions were doubtless of the best, but he was a stranger to the ways of broom handles. This one, in his hands, caught the lid of a kettle Norah had on the stove and sent it spinning across the room to land with a noisy clatter in the sink. Twaddles privately considered this a distinct feat, but Norah was unappreciative.

"Glory be! " cried the long-suffering Norah. "Be off with ye, and I'll clean up the mud. The more helpful ye try to be, Twaddles, the more work ye make. "

Twaddles departed with as much dignity as he could muster, and running through the front hall found his mother and his brother Bobby looking at the window boxes on the front porch. The boxes had been put away for the winter and that morning Father Blossom had brought them down to see about painting them.

"Can I plant things? " demanded Twaddles.

Meg, who was digging contentedly in the flower bed at the foot of the steps, looked at him sympathetically. Meg's fair little face was flushed and there was a streak of dirt across her small straight nose and she was unmistakably very busy and very happy.

"Isn't it fun? " she greeted her little brother. "Mother says we may each have a garden this year; didn't you, Mother? "

"I surely did, " agreed Mother Blossom, smiling. "What is Dot bringing? "

Around the corner of the house came Dot, Twaddles' twin sister. Her hair-ribbon drooped perilously on the end of a straggling lock of dark hair and her pretty dark blue frock hung in a gap below the belt where it had pulled loose at the gathers. Dot always had trouble about keeping her frocks neat.

"I got a hose! " she declared triumphantly. "Daddy won't have to buy one. The Mertons threw this out on the trash basket and I brought it home. I guess Daddy can mend it. "

Bobby shouted with laughter.

"That's the old piece they used to beat rugs with, " he said positively, "Nobody could mend that. "

"Come see the robin I found, " suggested Twaddles. "It's getting dry on the shelf warmer. Perhaps we can keep him to play with. "

"That you can't, " said Mother Blossom quickly. "It wouldn't be right in the first place, and in the second place it is against the law. You must put him out in the grass again, Twaddles, as soon as he is warm and dry. "

"Daddy! " Meg's quick eyes had seen a car making the corner turn. "Here comes Daddy! What color is the car, Bobby? "

"Black—no, blue, dark blue! " cried Bobby.

As the comfortable touring car drew up at the curb and the smiling driver waved a gloved hand at the eager group on the porch, Dot jumped up and down with excitement.

"Take me, Daddy? " she shrieked. "Aren't you going? "

Pell-mell the children raced down the garden path and Mrs. Blossom followed more leisurely.

"Aren't you going? " Dot kept repeating. "Aren't you going? "

"You don't care much where you go, do you, Dot? " asked her father whimsically. "The main idea with you seems to be to keep moving.

How about it, Mother—want to take a little drive? " Mrs. Blossom glanced toward the house.

"I'm as bad as the children, " she confessed. "It must be this Spring weather. I really ought to be upstairs mending stockings, but how can I stay indoors on a day like this? "

"Get your hat, " said Mr. Blossom crisply. "That settles it—we're going to take a spin. Pile in, youngsters. "

Mother Blossom came back with her hat and sweaters for the children, and Norah came to the door to wave to them and see the new car. It was a very handsome, nicely finished model, painted dark blue, as Bobby had said. The seats were upholstered in dark blue rep and there was plenty of room for the Blossom family and for guests, when they had them.

"May I ride with you, Daddy? " asked Meg.

"It's my turn, " insisted Twaddles. "Isn't it, Daddy? "

"That was the old car, " said Bobby. "This is beginning all over. Isn't it, Daddy? Meg and I should ride in the front seat first, 'cause we're the oldest. "

"If we have to hear this every time we go driving, I'm afraid Mother will refuse to go with us, " answered Father Blossom seriously. "Suppose we settle the question another time and to-day let the three girls ride in the tonneau? I'll need Bobby to keep an eye on Twaddles because I'll have to give all my attention to the wheel. "

"I know you must miss Sam, " said Mother Blossom, as Meg and Dot climbed in beside her and Bobby and Twaddles took their places in the front seat beside Father Blossom. "He was such an excellent driver. "

"Well, in a way, he kept me from learning, " said her husband, starting the car a trifle unevenly. "Sam was so fine a driver I was perfectly content to let him run the car and never even felt ambitious to drive myself. If we want to go anywhere this summer, I'll be glad I have my own driver's license. What's the matter, Twaddles? "

4

"I dropped my handkerchief, " announced Twaddles sadly. "Right in the mud. See? it's back there, Daddy. "

"Well, I hardly think we'll stop for that, " said Father Blossom judicially. "You've plenty of those little cotton things and I want to go as far as the lake road before supper time. "

"It wasn't a little cotton thing, " reported Twaddles, whose conscience was peculiar in that it usually bothered him too late. "I borrowed one of your nice, white hankies, Daddy, to wrap my sick bird in. "

"Well, I must say! " sputtered Father Blossom. "I must say! Oh, Twaddles, why do you always do something you shouldn't? Those handkerchiefs are pure linen and hand-initialed. I'll have to stop— you run back and see if you can find it. "

He stopped the car and Twaddles obediently jumped out and ran back to the place where he had dropped the handkerchief. When he had had plenty of time to return, and didn't appear, Bobby stood up in the car to look.

"He's fussing with something, " he announced. "He's got a stick and is poking something. I'd better go and get him, hadn't I, Daddy? "

"The child has probably found a garden snake or a frog, " said Mother Blossom, who knew her children thoroughly, as her next remark proved. "If Bobby goes after Twaddles they will play with it until dark. Let Meg go. Tell Twaddles, dear, that he is to come immediately. And don't let him forget the handkerchief. "

Meg ran all the way to where Twaddles sat on a stone blissfully engrossed with something in the roadway.

"Mother says to come this minute, " she commanded. "What you got, Twaddles? "

"There! you've scared it, " said Twaddles regretfully. "It was a dear little snake. All right, I'm coming. I was all ready to start when you came. "

After this delay the trip went smoothly, and Father Blossom declared that he was pleased with the new car. They reached the broad, level lake road and drove for several miles along it until Mother Blossom said that if they were not to keep Norah's supper waiting, they must turn back.

"Want to get out, Meg? " Father Blossom asked his little daughter gently.

Meg was always afraid when it was necessary to turn a car. She usually got out when Sam Layton, the Blossom's former chauffeur, backed their car or found a turn necessary. Now, however, she shook her head. Meg was learning, too.

Father Blossom carefully swung the heavy car around and was ready to send it ahead toward home when suddenly the wheel seemed to take matters into its own hand—if a steering wheel can do such a thing. Anyway, with a sudden lurch and a bound the car plunged directly into a heavy screen of brushwood that bordered one side of the road!

CHAPTER II

BOBBY HAS A PLAN

Twaddles was the first to speak. The plunge had been so unexpected and there had been so little warning, none at all, in fact, that if any one had been inclined to scream there was no opportunity. They were all breathless and rather shaken up. But Twaddles, who had thrown his arms around Bobby's neck, managed to grin.

"Well, what do you know about that! " he ejaculated in his funny, serious little voice.

That made them all laugh, and then Father Blossom began to ask anxiously if any one was hurt.

"No one, thank goodness, " Mother Blossom assured him, opening the tonneau door so that Meg and Dot might step out. "You haven't cut your hand, Ralph? "

"Just a scratch, " answered Father Blossom carelessly. "I bore down pretty hard on the wheel rim. Well, I'm thankful we didn't turn over. What do you suppose was the reason for this running jump? "

The four little Blossoms were out on the ground now, picking their way carefully, for they were surrounded by clumps of prickly bushes. Mother Blossom joined Father Blossom, who was anxiously inspecting the car.

"It's wedged in so tightly I'll never be able to back it out, " he said. "Only see, Margaret, how neatly it has slipped in between these three saplings. If I had tried that stunt I couldn't have made it once in fifty chances. "

Meg and Dot and Twaddles and Bobby crowded closer to look. Perhaps this is a good time to tell you who the four little Blossoms were, if you have never met them before.

You have guessed, of course, that they had other and longer names. Meg was named for her mother, Margaret; Bobby was Robert Hayward Blossom on the school roll; the twins (they were four years old) were Dorothy Anna and Arthur Gifford Blossom, but no one ever thought of calling the roly-poly dark-eyed pair anything but Dot and Twaddles.

If you have read the first book of this series, "Four Little Blossoms at Brookside Farm, " you know that Father Blossom owned a large foundry on the edge of the pretty town of Oak Hill and that he and his family lived in a comfortable old-fashioned house with Norah, who had been with them for years, and Sam Layton, the good-natured man of all work, to help make things run smoothly. You will remember that Brookside Farm was the name of Aunt Polly's home, Aunt Polly being the older sister of Mother Blossom. The Four Little Blossoms spent a delightful summer at Brookside and came home just in time for Meg and Bobby to enter Oak Hill school.

What they did that first winter in school and how the twins tried their best to do exactly as Meg and Bobby did, and usually succeeded, is told in the book called "Four Little Blossoms at Oak Hill School. " They found school most exciting and it did seem as though there was something to be done every minute of the short winter days, but, dear me, when the heavy snowfalls began you should have seen the children! They coasted, and they skated, and Meg lost her beautiful turquoise locket. But she found it, so you need not be sorry. The whole story of that locket is told in the third book of the series, called "Four Little Blossoms and Their Winter Fun. " Meg and Bobby were lost in a snowstorm, too, and for a time things looked very serious for them, but that adventure also had a happy ending.

And now we find the four little Blossoms, early in April, just as glad to see the beautiful, shining green Spring as they had been to see the first Winter snow. Sam Layton had gone away to Canada to work on a farm soon after the weather grew pleasant, and the four little Blossoms missed him very much. They suspected that Norah missed him, too, though she said nothing. The children had all promised to write to Sam, and Norah wrote every week.

This was the reason Father Blossom was driving the new car. As he said, Sam was such an excellent driver there had really been no need for him to drive; but with Sam away, if Father Blossom wanted to reach his foundry on time every morning there was nothing for him to do but to learn to drive the car himself.

8

"I'll go and see if I can persuade some farmer to come and pull us out, " he said to Mother Blossom, when he had tried without results to back the car from the mass of bushes and saplings into which it had driven. "You stay right here with Mother, children, and I'll be back in fifteen or twenty minutes. "

Twaddles wanted to go with his father, but when it was explained to him that his mother and the girls needed his protection and that of Bobby, he was quite willing to wait quietly in the bushes. That is, as quietly as Twaddles ever waited anywhere.

"Perhaps we can find flowers, " Meg suggested, as Father Blossom disappeared, whistling. "Brush some of these leaves away, Dot, and let's see what grows underneath. "

"Oh, dear! " came with a big sigh from Dot, and they turned to see her caught by a bush whose sharp spikes went right through her firm serge frock and bloomers and held her fast.

"I'll get you, " offered Twaddles gallantly, and he tried to scramble over the intervening bushes, fortunately all low.

But though low, they were tightly woven, for no underbrush had been cut from this section of the woods for years. In a moment Twaddles was pinned as tightly as Dot, a narrow, string-like coil of vine wrapping securely round his ankles and a sharp stake thrusting itself slantwise through the sleeve of his sweater.

"Don't wriggle, " implored Mother Blossom, as she and Meg and Bobby came cautiously to the rescue. "I do want these clothes to last you till it is time to buy Summer ones. Hold still, Dot. There! Now come and sit in the car and I'll tell you a story till Daddy comes back."

Bobby had managed to free Twaddles, and the four little Blossoms climbed into the car and really sat very still—for them—while Mother Blossom began the story of what she did when she was a little girl and went away to boarding school for the first time. The children loved "true" stories, and they listened intently till Dot spied her father coming down the crooked little path and set up a shout.

Father Blossom had found a farmer who lived near, and had arranged with him to bring two strong horses and a heavy rope and see if he could pull the car from the underbrush. The farmer was a tall, silent man who seemed not to hear the excited questions of the four little Blossoms, and never even spoke to Mother Blossom beyond a quick jerk at his cap when he first saw her sitting in the car.

But, although the farmer, whose name was Ellis, was "no talker" (he himself said so), he was a quick worker, and in less than ten minutes he had rigged up the rope to the car, fastened it to the collars of his horses, and in another five minutes the car was out in the road and clear of the bushes and saplings.

"Only scratched a mite, " commented the farmer, pocketing the bill Father Blossom gave him to pay for his time and trouble. "Lucky not to have to have the whole thing scraped and re-varnished. "

The Blossoms were home in time for supper, and of course Norah had to hear about the drive. Bobby did not have much to say, for he was busy thinking out a little plan that, he privately decided, could best be tried out at school. Bobby's experience had been that Twaddles and Dot always wanted a finger in his plans and that too many fingers are as bad as too many cooks. And any one will tell you that too many cooks are worse than none.

"Can I take my automobile to school this morning? " Bobby asked at the breakfast table the day after the drive in the new car.

Bobby was very proud of his automobile that worked with pedals like a tricycle but looked exactly like a miniature automobile, even to the red paint and the lamps and the tin license tacked on the back axle.

"If you won't let it interfere with your school work, I suppose you may, " conceded Mother Blossom. "Is there a place where you can keep it during school hours? "

"I can keep it down under the first floor stairs, " said Bobby eagerly. "And I won't play with it only before school and at recess, Mother, honest. "

So he was allowed to take the car, and he went early in order to have time for play before the nine o'clock bell. Meg hung on behind him and the twins watched them out of sight enviously. There was nothing in the world the twins desired so ardently as to go to school. They had been promised that they might start in the kindergarten the next term and they were already looking forward to that time.

"I want to play a new way, " Bobby was explaining to Meg as he pedaled furiously. "You'll see—I thought it up all myself last night. "

A crowd of boys swept forward to greet Bobby when he entered the school yard. Most of them had seen his car before—it had been a birthday present in February—but to several it was new and all admired it and wished for one exactly like it.

"Can't have any fun with it here, " said Tim Roon, rather contemptuously.

Tim was apt to speak of the dark side of everything, and he had very good luck in finding a dark side to draw attention to.

"Yes, I can, " insisted Bobby. "You'll see. "

He went through the school yard, down to the end where an old-fashioned picket fence shut off the playground from a vacant lot that later would be divided off into the school gardens, a plot for each grade.

"What you going to do? " asked Tim Roon curiously.

The other children looked mystified, including Meg. She, too, wondered what Bobby could be planning to do.

"You'll see. " Bobby repeated his favorite phrase.

From his blouse he drew a hammer, borrowed from the tool bench in the Blossom garage, and, awkwardly, for he was not used to the work, inserted it under the end of a picket. There was a ripping, grating noise, and the picket parted from the cross-piece.

11

"Bobby Blossom! " cried Meg. "What in the world are you going to do? "

CHAPTER III

HOW THE PLAN WORKED

"You'll see, " said Bobby with maddening persistency.

While the children watched, he ripped off four more pickets. The cross pieces of the fence were old and rotten and when he put his foot on the lower brace and bore down heavily, it obligingly snapped in two.

"I'm going to ride right through that hole! " Bobby condescended to explain at last. "Daddy drove our car right in between three trees, and I'll bet I can steer through a narrow place, too. You watch. "

Breathless the boys and girls stood back while Bobby pushed his automobile to a point he considered a proper distance from the opening in the fence. He took his seat, put his foot on the pedals, and tooted the horn.

"Here I go! " he cried, making his feet fly.

The car shot forward and, much to the surprise of every one except Bobby, went through the hole in the pickets safely and on out into the muddy lot.

"Pretty good steering, " said Palmer Davis generously.

"Let me try, " begged Meg. "I can steer, Bobby. "

Meg always did everything Bobby did, and it never entered his head to refuse her. So she took the automobile, and, holding the wheel tightly, pedaled through the hole, though more slowly than Bobby had done. Palmer Davis was wild to try his skill, but Meg insisted on two rides and when she had finished the second one the warning bell rang.

"You can have it the first thing recess, " promised Bobby to the disappointed Palmer, who felt better then and helped Bobby put the fascinating toy under the stairs in the back hall.

As soon as the recess bell sounded, Palmer and Bobby dashed down and out into the yard. Meg, who was a grade below them but in the same room, stayed behind to clean her desk, a favorite occupation with the little girls. Miss Mason, the teacher, was watering a shelf of plants, and the windows were all open to the lovely April sunshine. Meg hummed a little, she was so happy.

"Ow! Ow! " suddenly the most heart-breaking howl rose from the school yard, the cry of some one in great pain or sadly frightened.

"Some one is hurt! " cried Miss Mason, hurrying to the window that faced the playground.

"Ow! Ow! Ow! " louder and louder the shrieks rose.

"Can't be killed and make a noise like that, " said Miss Mason practically. "Can you tell who it is, Meg? "

Meg pushed aside one of the girls who stood in her way. She gave a glance from the window. She saw a crowd of boys surrounding the crying one and more boys hurrying from every part of the yard. The group parted for a moment and Meg glimpsed a bit of gleaming red tin. It was Bobby's automobile.

"It's Palmer! " Meg guessed instantly, "He must have hit the fence! "

She turned and ran from the room, leaving Miss Mason to reason out, if she could, what connection Palmer's howling had with hitting the fence.

Meg slid down the banisters, as the quickest way to reach the door, and was just in time to see Mr. Carter, the principal, run from his office out into the yard. Mr. Carter was really principal of the grammar school, where he spent most of his time, leaving the primary grades under the control of Miss Wright, the vice- principal. But he spent a certain number of days each month in the primary school office and the pupils soon discovered that he knew quite as well as Miss Wright what was going on in the lower grades.

"Oh, my! " gasped Meg as she sped after Mr. Carter. "I didn't know he was going to be here to-day. I wonder if Palmer is hurt much? "

Whether Palmer was badly hurt or not, he was certainly making a great noise. He continued to scream, "at the top of his lungs, " Norah would have said.

"Ow! Ow! " wailed Palmer. "Ow-wow! "

"Here, here, boy, nothing can be as bad as that sounds, " said Mr. Carter, pushing his way in among the children and stooping down to Palmer, who was huddled in a heap on the ground, his feet and the tin automobile apparently inextricably mixed. "Stand up, Palmer, and let me see where you are hurt. "

Palmer struggled to his feet, and Meg could see that he had a bump over one eye. The sleeve of his jacket was torn and his lip was bleeding slightly.

"Why, you're not so badly off, " Mr. Carter comforted him, taking his own handkerchief and wiping off the streaks left by tears and dirt on Palmer's round face. "No bones broken, laddie, and Miss Wright will fix that lip with a little court-plaster. She knows first-aid. What in the world were you doing down at this end of the yard? "

There was a sudden silence. Meg, on the outside of the crowd, experienced a distinctly uncomfortable feeling.

"Were you coasting, Palmer? " asked Mr. Carter, righting the automobile as he spoke. Then he saw the fence.

"Who ripped off those pickets? " he demanded sternly.

"I—I did, " admitted Bobby in a very small voice.

The clang of the gong sounded and Mr. Carter turned to the listening children.

"Go back to your classes, " he directed them. "You stay, Bobby and Palmer. I want to speak to you. "

Obediently the others filed in, not without many a backward glance at the group by the fence.

"Now suppose you tell me about it, " suggested Mr. Carter mildly.

So Bobby told about the drive of the previous afternoon and of how his father had landed the car in the bushes; he told about his scheme to prove that he could steer, and of how Palmer had asked to try, too.

"But he didn't make the hole wide enough, " complained the battered Palmer. "First try I hit the side. I think it's an awful silly thing to do, anyway. "

"Well, I went through without hitting anything! " said a voice unexpectedly. "You're always ready to make a fuss when you spoil a good game, Palmer. "

It was Meg. She had found it impossible to desert Bobby in trouble, and had come back in time to hear Palmer's grievance.

Mr. Carter tried not to smile.

"Aside from hurting Palmer, Bobby, " said the principal seriously, "you've damaged the school property. What do you suppose Mr. Hornbeck would say if he saw that fence? " Mr. Hornbeck was one of the school committeemen.

This was something Bobby had not considered.

"I'll mend it, " he promised hastily. "Honestly, I never thought about hurting the fence. "

"I know you didn't, " Mr. Carter said promptly. "Still, that really doesn't alter the fact that you've damaged property that doesn't belong to you. I think to help you remember another time, we'll say you must mend the fence this morning and make up the time after school. I'll take Palmer in and patch him up now. Meg, you should be in your classroom. "

"I want to help Bobby, " asserted Meg firmly. "I'll stay after school with him, too. It's just as much my fault—I knew he shouldn't pull off pickets, only I never told him. "

Mr. Carter looked at the little girl oddly.

"All right, only you'll have to make up the time with Miss Mason, " he said. "I think Bobby is a lucky boy to have such a loyal little sister."

Meg and Bobby managed to put the pickets back and Mr. Carter found a piece of new wood with which to patch the old cross piece. They learned that it is easier to destroy things than to mend them, and after they had stayed till half past four that night and Mother Blossom had heard the reason and forbidden them ever to take the tin automobile to school again, both children decided that a game with such a sorry ending wasn't worth planning.

The twins had spent the day grubbing in the garden. "Hunting grasshoppers, " Twaddles said, as Mother Blossom buttoned him into a clean blouse for supper.

"Why, it's months too early for grasshoppers, " said Meg scornfully. "They never come till it's hot in the summertime. How can you be so silly, Twaddles? "

"Huh! " was the best response Twaddles could make to this remark, but when he was ready to go downstairs he slipped into Meg's room. Her blue serge skirt and a fresh middy blouse lay over a chair and Twaddles knew she would wear them to school the next day. With a quick glance toward the door he slipped something into the pocket of the blouse, which was stitched into the turned up hem.

"Twaddles! " called Dot. "Twaddles! Hurry up. Mother says she wants to tell us something. Come on down. "

Mother Blossom was smiling as though something pleased her very much.

"Come into the living-room, children, " she said, as the four little Blossoms came running downstairs. "Daddy has telephoned that he won't be home to supper and we may take a few minutes to hear my news. Do you think you would like to go to Apple Tree Island? "

"Apple Tree Island? " repeated Twaddles, who never could keep still. "Is it a place, Mother? "

"A beautiful place, darling, " she assured him. "It has green grass and gray rocks and crooked old apple trees and is set down in the center of the prettiest lake you ever saw. "

"Who lives there, Mother? " asked Meg. "Are we going visiting? "

"Not exactly visiting, " explained Mother Blossom. "You know Daddy's friend, Mr. Winthrop? He owns a bungalow on Apple Tree Island, and this summer he and his family are going to England. He has told Daddy that we may have the use of this house if we care to go up to the lake. "

"Let's go! " cried Dot instantly. "Won't it be fun to live on an island like Robinson Crusoe? When are we going, Mother? "

Mother Blossom laughed.

"That is for Daddy to say, " she answered. "I'm not sure that we are really going. "

CHAPTER IV

TWADDLES' GRASSHOPPER

Apple Tree Island was the main topic of conversation at the table that night. The four little Blossoms were wildly excited at the prospect of going on an island to live, and Twaddles had a secret idea that one swam out to it from the mainland.

"I haven't told you the very nicest part of the plan, " said Mother Blossom, as she served the pudding. "If we go, and mind you, children, nothing is definitely settled yet, Daddy will drive us in the new car and we'll stop at Brookside to see Aunt Polly! "

They were all in bed long before Father Blossom came home, and the next morning Meg and Bobby hurried off to school, leaving the twins to talk about the proposed trip.

"I'll tell you the story of Apple Tree Island to-night, " Father Blossom had promised them at breakfast. "I think I can safely say that we will go in a week or so, or as soon as Mother can get you ready and make her plans. I have to get some equipment for the car, too. "

So there was a story connected with this island which had such a pretty name! No wonder the four little Blossoms thought it must be a wonderful place. They were so anxious to be off that it seemed to them they simply could not be patient for two long weeks.

"But school doesn't close—not until the middle of May! " Meg voiced this distressing thought when she and Bobby were at the Oak Hill school door. "Oh, Bobby, wouldn't it be awful if every one went to Apple Tree Island except us! "

Bobby insisted that such a dreadful thing wasn't to be thought of, but the idea troubled him all through the morning session. At noon, for he and Meg went home to lunch, he asked Mother Blossom whether she thought he and Meg would be left out of the island plan because of the fact that school would still be in session when the Blossoms started.

"Why, my dear little son, what a notion! " cried Mother Blossom, kissing him warmly. "As if we could be happy two seconds without you and Meg! Daddy and I talked it over, and we decided, before I told you children of the plan, that if we had to go before school closed it wouldn't be such a serious matter, because you both have had excellent reports and the last school month is given over to review work. If you and Meg have been attentive throughout the term, and Miss Mason says you have, you can afford to miss a few weeks. "

Bobby was immensely relieved and looked over at Meg to see if she did not share his pleasure. Meg, however, was scowling at Twaddles, who seemed decidedly uncomfortable.

"Mother! " Meg had been waiting for her mother's attention. "Mother, you ought to see what Twaddles did to me this morning. "

Bobby suddenly snickered.

"Oh, Mother, " he giggled, "it was the funniest thing you ever saw! It hopped right across Bertrand Ashe's foot and Meg went to pick it up and it went, plop! into Palmer Davis's inkwell. Miss Mason thought Meg did it on purpose. "

"What hopped? " asked Mother Blossom, mystified. "And Meg, why are you frowning so at poor Twaddles? "

"He knows, all right, " declared Meg wrathfully. "He put that jumping grasshopper Aunt Polly sent him in my middy blouse pocket. And it mortified me very much, Mother. "

"I don't doubt it, Daughter, " said Mother Blossom sympathetically. "Twaddles, I think that was rather a mean trick. "

"Paid her up for calling me silly, " muttered Twaddles, his face scarlet.

"It was funny, though, " insisted Bobby smiling.

Meg tried not to laugh and then she gave in.

"Yes, it was, " she admitted, dimpling. "The ink splashed all over, Mother, and when Miss Mason made Palmer take it out it gave another jump and landed way over on the window seat. "

"Miss Mason has it now, " said Bobby. "She wouldn't give it back. "

"But it's mine, " wailed Twaddles. "I want it to play with. Make Meg get it, won't you, Mother? "

"I won't! " announced Meg stubbornly.

"Don't speak that way, Meg, " said Mother Blossom gently. "Twaddles, it seems to me that since the grasshopper got Meg into such trouble, and you put it in her pocket, that you're the one to get it back. If you want it badly enough to ask Miss Mason for it, well and good; otherwise I fear you have lost your grasshopper. "

Poor Twaddles knew there was no way out of it. Either he must lose his beautiful green grasshopper, or else go and ask Miss Mason to give it to him. Mother Blossom never allowed the children to coax; when she said a thing she always meant it.

"Will you go ask, Dot? " Twaddles said to his little sister, after Meg and Bobby had gone back to school.

"I'll go with you, " offered Dot "But I won't go all by myself without any one with me. "

So it happened that Miss Mason was much surprised to receive a visit that afternoon a few minutes after she had dismissed her class. She had met Twaddles and Dot before, when they had paid their first visit to the school, and she remembered them at once.

"I'm very glad to see you, " she assured them. "Won't you come in and sit down? Meg and Bobby have been telling me about Apple Tree Island. "

"Yes, I guess we're going, " murmured Twaddles, his eyes fixed in fascination on his mechanical grasshopper reposing on the top of the teacher's desk.

21

"Will Norah and Annabel Lee and Philip go with you? " asked Miss Mason, who knew all about the Blossom family and their pets.

"I don't know about Norah and Annabel Lee, " returned Dot politely, "but Sam Layton took Philip to Canada with him; he was really like Sam's own dog 'cause he mostly fed him. Of course, " she added, "that makes Twaddles very lonesome. "

"Yes? " said Miss Mason, as though she did not quite understand.

"You see, " explained Dot bravely, "now he hasn't any dog or any grasshopper! "

Miss Mason stared at the little girl for a moment. Then she leaned back in her chair and laughed.

"Is that your grasshopper, Twaddles? " she asked merrily. "What was it doing, then, in Meg's pocket? "

Miss Mason had at first refused to use any nicknames in her class and she had insisted on calling Bobby and Meg by their true names, "Robert" and "Margaret. " As for Twaddles and Dot, the teacher had declared that never, never, could she consent to calling children by such "queer" names. But, after a while, she had grown used to the queer names and, like every one else in Oak Hill, forgot that the four little Blossoms had any others.

Dot sensibly thought that Twaddle should make his own explanation, and that small boy did, rather shamefacedly. Miss Mason gave him his grasshopper and advised him not to play tricks on his sister again.

"I won't, " promised Twaddles earnestly, "at least, not pocket ones. "

Down in the hall, on their way out, Twaddles and Dot met Mr. Carter, who also remembered them from their earlier visit. He shook hands with them and very naturally asked them what brought them to school.

"Meg and Bobby went home at least half an hour ago, " he said kindly.

"We came for my grasshopper, " explained Twaddles, and that brought out the whole story.

"Dot, " remarked Twaddles thoughtfully when they were walking home, "it wouldn't be so bad being bad if you didn't have to tell about it, would it? "

Dot understood at once.

"N—o, " she drawled slowly. "But we'd feel worse if we never did tell. "

Twaddles was so glad to get his grasshopper back that he made it hop all the way home. And at home the twins found Miss Florence, the Oak Hill dressmaker, talking with Mother Blossom.

"I'll come to-morrow, then, " Miss Florence was saying as Dot and Twaddles came up the path. "Here's Dot now. Come here, child, while I measure your skirt. Did you know you were going to have a new dress to wear to Apple Tree Island? "

"I hope it's pink, " said Dot with interest. "Pink with a white organdie sash. And I can wear my white shoes and stockings. "

"When can we begin to pack? " demanded the practical Bobby. "We can do most of that for you, Mother. "

Miss Florence folded up her measure.

"Your mother's going to have her hands full, " she observed, rising. "Well, it's most supper time and I must run. I'll be over early in the morning, Mrs. Blossom. Here comes Mr. Blossom now. "

"Tell us the story! " cried the four little Blossoms, falling upon their father before he had brought the car quite to a stop. "Tell us the story about Apple Tree Island, Daddy! Please! "

"With fresh asparagus for supper? " asked Father Blossom in great surprise. "I couldn't think of it! After supper you shall hear all about the island, chicks. "

CHAPTER V

APPLE TREE ISLAND

"Now tell us, Daddy, " begged Dot when, supper over, they were gathered about the fireplace in the living room. "Tell us, 'fore Twaddles and I have to go to bed. "

"It isn't such a long story, " began Father Blossom. "You can hear it all before you have to go to bed. I don't know whether Mother has told you, but when Bobby was a baby we spent a summer on Apple Tree Island. "

"It's funny I don't seem to remember much about it, " remarked Bobby anxiously.

"Well, old man, not so funny considering that you were about eight months old, " returned his father with a smile. "We rented a rather pretty cottage very near the spot where Mr. Winthrop, a year or so later, built his bungalow. Your mother started off for a walk one day with Bobby, and she walked too far; he was heavy for a baby, and she should never have tried to carry him. But she did, and she walked as far as the other end of the island before her strength gave out. Then what do you suppose she did, Meg? "

Meg looked serious.

"I don't know, " she admitted. "Maybe she cried? "

"Mothers don't cry, " said Twaddles in fine scorn. "Do they, Daddy?"

"I cried, " confessed Mother Blossom, smiling at the astonished Twaddles. "I'll never forget how I felt—so far from home and with a heavy, fretting baby in my arms. I just sat down on a rock and cried. And Bobby cried with me. "

The four little Blossoms were too amazed to speak. To think of Mother crying!

24

"Pretty soon some one came along the road, " Father Blossom went on with the story, "and, of course, they saw Mother and Bobby crying. This some one was a woman in a gray wrapper, pushing a baby carriage in which were two little children and a great many packages. The children were two boys about three and four years old, and the woman was their mother. She said her name was Mrs. Harley and that she lived about a quarter of a mile further on. She was very good indeed to Mother—made her little boys get out and walk and put Bobby in with the bundles. Then she helped Mother as far as her house, gave her hot tea and some bread and butter, and kept her until Mr. Harley came home. He had a rickety old buggy and a shabby horse and he harnessed up and brought Mother and Bobby home in great style. "

"That was nice, " said Meg with satisfaction. "Can we go and see Mrs. Harley when we get to Apple Tree Island? "

"There is no Mrs. Harley there now, " answered Father Blossom almost sadly. "She came to see Mother several times that summer. Mr. Harley was shiftless and easy going, but extremely fond of his family. They lived in a shack, but they loved each other devotedly and that, you know, is much better than having a fine house. Well, Mother never went to Apple Tree Island again—you youngsters kept her too busy. But I went nearly every year because I've always had to look after some property there for an invalid friend of Aunt Polly's. I never went that I didn't see the Harleys and carry them some message or gift from Mother. Four years ago Mrs. Harley met me with the news that her husband had disappeared. "

"Was he drowned? " asked Twaddles fearfully.

"No, no one thought so, " answered Father Blossom. "Mrs. Harley said that he had been acting queerly all that Winter—that he would go for days without speaking, and then fly into a rage if any one asked him a question. " "He was always so good to his family, " said Mother Blossom, smoothing Meg's hair absently. "He must have been out of his mind, Ralph. "

"I think so myself, " agreed Father Blossom. "Anyway, Mrs. Harley told me that one morning, a wet, cold day in March, he got up before it was light, lit a fire in the kitchen stove and went out of the house. They never saw him again. He had a rowboat and this they found abandoned on the south shore of Sunset Lake, showing that he must have rowed over to the mainland.

"The next summer, when I went to Apple Tree Island, I was told that Mrs. Harley and the children had also disappeared, " continued Father Blossom. "She had gone, leaving no trace, and taking the two little boys with her. I went to see the shack and she had left it as neat as wax inside and not one scrap of paper anywhere to give a clue as to what she intended to do. "

"Polly saw her after that, " Mother Blossom reminded him.

"Yes, that's so, she did, " agreed Father Blossom. "She stopped there one afternoon and Aunt Polly tried to keep her over night; but she was anxious to begin her journey and would not even stay to supper."

The hall clock struck eight.

"Oh, dear, " sighed Dot. "Just as things get exciting we always have to go to bed! "

"That's the whole story! " announced Father Blossom, pulling her down into his lap for a kiss. "There's no more to tell, chicken, if you should stay up till midnight to listen. No one knows what became of the Harley family, and I believe their shack is slowly falling to pieces. I haven't been to the Island for two summers— not since Mrs. Harley went off, in fact. And now don't let Mother have to tell you twice what time it is if you want to be invited to ride in the front seat with me on the trip to Aunt Polly's. "

"Wouldn't you like to know where they went? " sleepily murmured Dot, toiling upstairs after Mother Blossom and Twaddles. "Wouldn't you, Mother? "

"Very much, " said Mother Blossom promptly. "Mrs. Harley was so kind to me, always, and we liked the whole family. I only hope she had relatives who could help her with the children. "

The next morning Miss Florence came with her needle and thread in the little leather case she always carried, and Dot, in the importance of being fitted for a new frock, quite forgot to envy Meg and Bobby, who hurried to school.

Father Blossom came home from the foundry early that afternoon, and when Dot and Twaddles heard him tinkering in the garage, they ran out to see what he was doing.

"What's the little gate for, Daddy? " asked Twaddles.

"To keep the suitcases on the running board, " explained Father Blossom, busy attaching the "gate" to the car.

"Don't we take a trunk? " Dot wanted to know, managing to tip over the box of screws.

"We'll ship those by express, " explained Father Blossom. "Look out, Dot, you'll step in that can of grease next. What's that hanging from you—here, turn around and let me see. "

Sure enough, a long strip of white muslin was streaming from under Dot's petticoat.

"Dear me, " exclaimed that small person in surprise, "I guess that's the petticoat Miss Florence basted a ruffle on. I must have forgotten to take it off. "

"She's calling you now, " announced Twaddles. "You go on in. I'll stay and help Daddy. "

"Well, do you know, " said Father Blossom respectfully, "while I'm very much obliged to you, I think there's nothing you can do for me just at present. Can't you do something for Mother or Norah? "

"Norah's ironing, " Twaddles answered disconsolately. "She says I make her nervous when she's ironing. And Mother is helping make Dot a dress. "

"I'll tell you, " cried Father Blossom. "How would you like to do a little packing for me? You would? That's fine. Down cellar you'll find an old basket; you take that up to my room and put everything you find in the lowest desk drawer into it. Then I'll carry it down

27

when I come in. The lowest drawer, remember. I've been wanting to clear that out for a long, long time, and I mustn't go away on a trip and leave that trash there. "

"Dot! Dot! " called Norah. "Your mother says you should come right away. "

Dot scuttled for the house, and Twaddles, delighted with the idea of helping his father, ran to find the basket. Dot was securely pinned into her new frock when he came panting upstairs, and she implored him to wait until she could help pack, too. Twaddles generously consented, and Mother Blossom warned them not to touch anything except the one desk drawer. They promised, and when Dot had resumed her old dress, without the basted petticoat, they earnestly set to work.

"What a lot of stuff! " exclaimed Dot, turning over a rusty bolt curiously. "What's this for, Twaddles? "

"I don't know, " said Twaddles. "Don't putter, Dot. Mother says the way to get a job done is to work steadily. "

Thus admonished, Dot put both her hands in and brought up a quantity of old papers mixed with bits of string, little ends of sealing wax and many other things she would have liked to stop and examine if Twaddles had not been the foreman.

There was a good deal of dust and loose dirt in the drawer, which had been waiting for Father Blossom to put in order for months, and Twaddles, who was really a neat little workman, brought a newspaper, after they had the drawer cleared out, and spread it on the floor. Then he tipped the empty drawer over this and all the dirt and dust was caught on the paper.

"Now that's done, " he announced with satisfaction, folding up the paper and stuffing it on top of the already full basket. "I'll put the drawer back and then I'll carry the basket down to the cellar. "

"Daddy said he'd take it, " objected Dot.

"But he'll be glad to find I've done it, " said Twaddles confidently. "Look out, Dot—push that paper down. Gee! it is kind of heavy. "

He staggered off toward the stairway, the basket in his arms. He had filled it so full that he could not see over the top and, just as he reached the head of the stairs, his foot caught in a rug. The basket pitched forward, but Twaddles caught the banister rail and saved himself from falling.

"Glory be! " Loud rose the wail of Norah, who was in the lower hall on her way upstairs with a pile of clean sheets. "Glory be, what's all this dirt raining on my clean front stairs! "

CHAPTER VI

ERRANDS IN TOWN

Well, accidents will happen, and after all no one scolded very much. To be sure, the dust and dirt and screws and rusty bolts and little pieces of paper were pretty thoroughly scattered about the hall and on the stairs, but Twaddles and Dot worked like beavers to pick them up. And Norah was so glad that Twaddles had not tumbled with the basket that she did not grumble at having to brush the stairs down for the second time that day. Father Blossom understood that Twaddles was trying to surprise him, so he did not scold when he came in from the garage and heard what had happened. And, really, Annabel Lee was the most injured. Not only were her nerves startled by the racket (she had been curled up asleep on the newel post, a favorite resting place of hers) but a long nail had rapped her smartly on the sensitive tip of her cat nose. Annabel Lee found it hard to forgive Twaddles for that performance.

When Meg and Bobby came in from school they were eager to help, too, and Mother Blossom was glad to have a list of errands to be done in town ready for them. Somehow, the four little Blossoms filled a house very full at times.

"We're going a week from Monday, " said Meg, skipping along beside Bobby, while the twins, "counting stones, " followed.

Counting stones was a favorite game of Dot and Twaddles. Every third one they had to walk around and sometimes it took them a long time to get to the town because there were so many stones to count.

"An' after Friday we won't have to go to school, " said Bobby.

"A week from Friday, " corrected Meg. "I wish we could stay at home all the time like Dot and Twaddles. Have you Mother's list, Bobby? "

Bobby had the list in his pocket and there were really a number of things to be done.

"You hold the bag, " Meg directed, "and I'll buy the things. "

So Bobby held the bag and Meg did the shopping and the twins poked their short, freckled noses into all the boxes and baskets they came to.

The last errand was at the grocery store, and there were three or four people ahead of the four little Blossoms. Meg waited quietly, and Bobby was interested in watching the big machine that ground coffee, but the irrepressible twins wandered off to investigate the long row of bins with sliding covers that filled one side of the store.

"Now Meg, " said the good-natured young clerk, when he had finished weighing out three pounds of prunes and two and a half pounds of rice for a fussy customer who changed her mind three times before she finally gave her order, "what can I do for you? "

"Mother wants a box of oatmeal, half a pound of mixed tea, and a pound of lump sugar, " announced Meg importantly.

"Right-o! " declared the clerk, taking a long hook pole from the counter and starting for the other side of the store where the package goods were kept on the upper shelves.

Just as he reached the shelves, Meg called to him.

"Oh, Mr. Carroll, " she began, meaning to ask him to bring a box of cornstarch, something Mother had written across the bottom of the list and which Bobby had overlooked when he read the list to Meg.

The clerk turned, his pole upraised, and Dot, who had been hanging over a flour bin nearly empty, slipped. Her feet flew up, her head went down, and she tripped the grocery clerk. His long pole crashed into the neat pile of boxes arranged on the shelves and a shower of oatmeal, cornstarch, macaroni and other cereals fell in an avalanche.

"I knew you'd do it, " scolded Bobby, rushing forward, though of course he couldn't have known that Dot meditated such a catastrophe. In fact, that small girl was more surprised than any one else.

"I was just a-looking, " she wept, when they pulled her out by her feet and she stood revealed with flour on her face and well rubbed into her dark hair and eyebrows, to say nothing of the hair- ribbon. "I was just a-looking in. "

"There, there, I guess we're all right, " stout Mr. Eustice, who owned the store, consoled her. "See, Dot, you're not hurt and Carroll here fell on a sack of grain which didn't break his bones. Not even one box is smashed, so why shed tears? 'Tisn't every little girl comes to see us who can say she's been in the flour bin. "

Dot continued to sob while Mr. Carroll did up the oatmeal and the cornstarch and the other things and put them in Bobby's bag. She was still crying when the four little Blossoms went down the grocery store steps and turned toward the road that led home.

"I should think you would cry, " said Meg severely. "I was so mortified! Can't you go anywhere, Dot, without falling into something? "

"Don't rub it in, " whispered Bobby, feeling sorry for his little sister. Then he happened to get a good look at Twaddles, who had been suspiciously quiet ever since Dot's unfortunate accident.

"Twaddles Blossom! " ejaculated Bobby. "What have you sat in? "

Twaddles twisted anxiously, trying to get a look at the back of his tunic blouse and bloomers.

"Does it show? " he asked uncomfortably. "I thought perhaps it didn't. I don't know what it is, Bobby—I only sat on that little box by the pump-thing in the back of the store. "

"That's where they fill the kerosene oil cans, " Bobby informed him. "I guess you've gone and soaked up some of the oil. Don't go near a match or you'll burn up. "

This awful prospect alarmed Twaddles beyond words.

"I'll stay out here, " he quavered nervously, for by this time the four little Blossoms had reached their own front lawn. "Mother might have the fireplace lighted. "

Meg and Dot and Bobby were relieved at Twaddles' decision. They had no wish to see their little brother catch fire, and fire they always associated with kerosene oil, thanks to Norah's repeated and solemn warnings.

No one missed Twaddles until they were seated at the table.

"Where's Twaddles? " asked Mother Blossom in some alarm as she noted his empty chair. "Didn't he go to the store with you, Bobby? "

"Yes, Mother, he went with us, " answered Bobby composedly, beginning to taste his soup.

"I wonder if he's upstairs washing his hands, " went on Mother Blossom. "Dot, will you run and call him? "

"He isn't upstairs, " said Dot quickly.

Mother Blossom stared, bewildered.

"Didn't he come back with you? " she asked.

"Oh, yes, he came back, " admitted Bobby. "Didn't he, Meg? "

Meg nodded, but said nothing. All three of the children had a vague idea that they were doing Twaddles a great kindness. Of course Mother Blossom would not be pleased to find that he had sat down in kerosene oil.

"Ralph! " said Mother Blossom in an odd, choked voice. "Oh, Ralph—"

"Bobby, where is Twaddles? " demanded Father Blossom sternly. "Where did you leave him? Is anything the matter with him? "

"He's outdoors, " said Bobby desperately. "I don't think anything much is the matter with him, Daddy. "

"Outdoors? " echoed Mother Blossom in wonder. "Why doesn't he come in? "

"He can't, " said Dot earnestly.

"Why can't he? " asked Father and Mother Blossom in chorus.

Bobby and Meg and Dot saw that they could no longer shield Twaddles.

"He can't come in, " blurted Bobby, "because he sat down where they fill oil cans in the grocery store and the back of him is all kerosene oil and he'll catch fire and burn up if he stays in the house."

Mother Blossom looked at Father Blossom, who sat perfectly still for a moment. Then he put back his head and shouted. He laughed until the tears ran down his face and Norah came in to see what the matter was.

"Don't laugh, " urged Mother Blossom. "Go and bring the poor child in, Ralph. "

"In a minute, " Father Blossom promised. "I want to get this straight first. Do you mean to tell me, Bobby, that you left Twaddles outdoors because you were afraid he would catch fire? How long did you expect him to stay there? "

"Well, we didn't know, " admitted Bobby lamely. "I guess it will wear off by morning. "

Father Blossom wiped his eyes and laid down his napkin.

"I'll go and get him, " he said, rising. "Mother, I begin to think an island is the only place for a family such as ours. There's one thing I don't suppose occurred to you, Bobby. "

"What, Daddy? " asked Bobby seriously.

"That Twaddles might have taken off his oil-soaked suit, " replied Father Blossom, going to the rescue of the lonely and hungry little fellow.

Meg and Bobby and Dot looked at each other.

"I never thought of that, " confessed Bobby.

CHAPTER VII

BEGINNING THE JOURNEY

"There's Tim Roon! Wave to him, Bobby, " cried Meg.

"Doesn't Marion Green look funny before she knows you? " commented Dot.

The car with Mother and Father Blossom and the four little Blossoms and their suitcases and rugs and shawls and long and short coats, had whirled past Marion Green so rapidly that she had not guessed who the people were until they were almost around the corner, though she waved to them in answer to their call.

For the time at last had come to start for Apple Tree Island, and this morning the Blossoms were actually on their way. Norah's sister had come to stay with her and Annabel Lee, so Mother Blossom had been spared the work and trouble of closing the house. Meg and Bobby had been promised that they could go into a higher grade in the fall, because of their good records for the term. Dot's new dresses were all finished; and Twaddles had wheedled his father into allowing him to take along an empty bird-cage which took up a great deal of room and was utterly useless. The Blossoms had no bird, and, as Bobby pointed out to Twaddles, he would not be able to catch a bird if he tried, and if he did catch one, said Bobby, it would be against the law for him to keep it. He would have to let it go as he had the robin. But Twaddles was firm in his resolve to carry the empty cage.

"Miss Florence's canary bird died, " he explained to Father Blossom. "And it makes her cry to see the cage; so she gave it to me. I think it is very nice and you never can tell when it will be useful! "

It was over seventy miles to Apple Tree Island from Oak Hill, quite too long a trip for the children to make without a break. This was partly the reason Father Blossom planned to stop at Brookside Farm. The real reason, of course, was Aunt Polly.

"When do we go on the boat? " asked Dot, soon after they had left Oak Hill and were running smoothly along the State highway which the interurban trolley line followed for some distance. Dot remembered the trip on the boat to Aunt Polly's, and she had reason to, as you will recall if you have read of that memorable visit.

"We don't go on the boat, " answered Mother Blossom. "We go as far as Little Havre, at the lower end of Lake Tobago, where we took the boat, and then we branch off and follow the lake shore road that brings us straight to Brookside Farm and Aunt Polly. "

"I dropped my cage, " announced Twaddles conversationally.

Of course there was nothing to do but stop the car and let him get out and run back for it. Father Blossom was a skillful driver now and there was no danger that the steering wheel would play him strange tricks.

Presently it was lunch time, and as Father and Mother Blossom had foreseen that traveling in the balmy Spring air and sunshine might sharpen appetites, they had arranged to have a picnic under the largest and shadiest tree that could be found. How glad the four little Blossoms were to get out of the car and run about on the grass, and how good Norah's sandwiches did taste! There was milk for the children, and coffee for Father and Mother, and after the meal was finished, Father Blossom showed the children how to bury the papers and waste so that the pretty meadow spot might not be spoiled for the next picnic party.

"Where are we going to have supper? " speculated Dot, as she snuggled into the car beside Mother Blossom. Dot was a great girl to consider the future.

"Can't you guess? " teased Mother Blossom.

"I know! " cried Meg. "Aunt Polly's. "

Dot and Twaddles enjoyed a little nap that sunny afternoon, but Meg and Bobby were wide awake every instant. When they came to Little Havre the twins awoke and sat up, a bit heavy-eyed, but inclined to be resentful that they had missed anything at all.

"There's the wharf! " shouted Twaddles. "'Member the organ-grinder man, Dot? And there's the restaurant where you spilled the milk on your dress. "

"I want to get a few directions, " said Father Blossom, running the car close to the curb under a drooping willow tree. "Don't get out, any one, for I'll be right back. "

He disappeared into the real-estate office on the corner, and the four little Blossoms amused themselves by watching the people hurrying down to make the afternoon boat.

"We'll beat them, won't we, Mother? " asked Meg. "And this time Aunt Polly won't have to come to meet us. "

Father Blossom came hurrying back and climbed into his seat.

"I'm glad I asked, " he told Mother Blossom. "They're repairing a stretch of the lake shore road and we'll have to make a short detour. It won't add more than half an hour to our running time. "

They moved forward slowly, for the narrow streets of the little town observed no traffic rules, and boat passengers, baby carriages, horses, jitneys and automobiles had to find their way about as best they could, and then, when they reached the open road, Father Blossom allowed his car to gather more speed.

"Isn't the lake pretty! " said Meg, as they rounded a curve and saw the water shining through the screen of trees. "What do you suppose they are doing in that funny boat? "

"Fishing, aren't they, Daddy? " Bobby asked. "I hope I can go fishing. Palmer Davis went with his father twice last year. "

"I'll take you, " Father Blossom promised.

"There's a man walking, " Dot announced suddenly.

Before any one could stop him, Twaddles had mounted his seat, his precious cage under his arm.

"Where? " he demanded.

Then he lost his balance and the cage shot over the side of the car.

"Oh, dear, " sighed Twaddles. "I didn't mean to drop it, Daddy. Honestly, it slipped. "

Father Blossom looked rather grim, for his patience with the useless cage was sorely tried.

"I'll get it, " shouted the solitary walker, who had turned on hearing the car and now ran back toward the Blossoms.

He was a pleasant-faced man, rather shabbily dressed, with a soft felt hat pulled well down over honest gray eyes. He handed the cage up to Twaddles smiling and revealing a set of square, even white teeth. Father Blossom started as the light fell clearly across the man's face.

"Dick Harley! " he ejaculated. "Where did you drop from? "

The man pushed his hat back and his smile changed to a slow, sheepish grin. His hair was quite gray at the temples and Meg privately decided that he must be old.

"Well, well, Mr. Blossom! " he exclaimed, plainly pleased. "You're the last person I ever expected to meet right here. This your family? "

"Get in, if you're going our way, " said Father Blossom cordially. "Margaret, you remember Dick Harley? "

Mother Blossom held out her hand.

"Of course I do, though it has been several years since we've seen each other, " she said pleasantly. "Oh, there's plenty of room, Mr. Harley. You sit with Mr. Blossom and I'll take Dot on my lap. "

Dot was passed over the back seat, and Mr. Harley sat in the front seat with Twaddles between him and Father Blossom.

"This your family? " he repeated. "Which is the little feller I used to hold in my lap? "

"That was Bobby, " smiled Mother Blossom. "He's seven years old now. This is Meg, and the two youngsters are our twins, Twaddles

38

and Dot. We're going to Apple Tree Island. I have never been back since—"

She stopped, afraid that perhaps she had recalled painful memories to Mr. Harley. But his attractive smile slowly overspread his face again.

"That so? " he said with interest. "I haven't been there myself in quite a spell. I expect the boys have grown out of sight. I'm on my way now to see the wife and kids. "

The Blossom family remained perfectly silent. What could they say?

CHAPTER VIII

OLD BROOKSIDE FRIENDS

"Yes, " repeated Mr. Harley comfortably. "I don't suppose the boys will know me. Dick must be ten now, and Herbert's a year older. I calculate to stay over to-night with Joe Gates and his wife in Pomona (that's why you folks overtook me walking along this road) and he'll row me up to the island. "

The four little Blossoms wriggled uneasily. Even Dot and Twaddles, young as they were, could guess something of what Mr. Harley's sorrow would be when he learned that no wife and children waited for his coming on pretty Apple Tree Island. Meg glanced at Mother Blossom. That lady shook her head slightly, as a signal not to speak.

"Isn't that a sign of spring water for sale? " said Father Blossom suddenly. "Hand me the vacuum bottles, Margaret, please, and I'll have them filled. The children may be thirsty again before we get to Polly's. Dick, will you help me? We've a bottle for each youngster and they're slippery things to handle. "

Father Blossom stopped the car on the other side of the road from a pretty cottage where a sign on the gate offered "Guaranteed, Analyzed Spring Water for Sale, " and he and Mr. Harley disappeared with the bottles through the odd, rustic gate.

"Now he'll tell the poor man, " sighed Mother Blossom. "Whatever they do or say when they come back, children, I don't want you to say a word unless you're spoken to. Can you remember? "

"Yes'm, " promised the four little Blossoms, four little hearts warm with sympathy for poor Mr. Harley.

"Where do you suppose he was all the time he wasn't there? " whispered Meg.

"I don't know, " answered her mother. "He may have been ill. He may not even know how long it has been since he has been home. Anyway, darlings, the kindest thing we can do is not to bother him with talk or questions. "

Father Blossom and Mr. Harley were gone for what seemed a long time to the children, but in reality was not more than twenty minutes. The four little Blossoms saw them coming, Father Blossom in the lead. Such a change had come over Mr. Harley! His shoulders sagged, he scuffed his feet and his eyes were heavy and dull.

"I suppose you know? " he said wearily to Mother Blossom, as he climbed into the car and Father Blossom took the wheel. "If I only knew where she went! But she quarreled with her people when she married me, and I never rightly knew where they lived, or who they were. "

"You'll probably find her, " Mrs. Blossom tried thus to encourage him. "It isn't easy for a woman with two children to drop out of sight, you know. Some one will be able to give you a clue. "

Mr. Harley shook his head despondently.

"It's been two years, your husband tells me, " he replied. "And I've been missing for four. Like as not she doesn't want to see me. I was out o' my mind for three years, Ma'am, and when I came to I was in a hospital on the California coast. It took me a year to work my way East. I kept writing and writing and wondering why Lou didn't send me a line. She was never one to bear a grudge. "

"But what will you do? " asked Mrs. Blossom, her kind eyes filling with tears as she pictured the ruined little shack on the island. "Don't go back there and try to live, Mr. Harley—it will only make you ill again. You know Mrs. Harley isn't there, and I can not bear to think of you there alone. "

"I'll stay to-night in Pomona, " said Mr. Harley slowly. "Then I'll go on to Sunset Lake and put up a while with Chris Smith; he owns a boathouse and I can earn my keep taking folks about the lake. I'll be on the spot then if she should come back or if any one comes with news of her. And if your sister knows where she went—"

"We'll ask her to-night and tell you as soon as we reach Sunset Lake, " promised Mother Blossom heartily.

The rest of the drive was accomplished almost in silence, Mr. Harley busy with his own brooding thoughts and the Blossoms anxious not

41

to annoy him. When they reached the town of Pomona, they left him at the post-office, where he said Joe Gates was always to be found. Another five miles brought the Blossoms to Brookside Farm.

"There's Foots! " shouted Twaddles, standing up on the seat and waving to Aunt Polly, who came flying down the drive.

"And Linda! " cried Meg.

"And Jud! And Peter Apgar! " shrieked Bobby.

"My darling lambs! " babbled Aunt Polly, almost beside herself with pleasure. "I never was so glad to see any one in all my life! Margaret, you look positively beautiful! Ralph, Jud will show you where to drive the car in. Oh, isn't this the nicest thing that ever happened to us, Linda? "

Linda smiled happily and nodded. She had grown taller since the four little Blossoms had seen her and she wore her hair pinned up in a pretty knot on top of her head.

Still laughing and talking, Aunt Polly marshaled her guests into the house. The twins were so sleepy from the long ride that they could hardly keep their eyes open, but they insisted on coming to the supper table. Linda and Aunt Polly had spent hours over that supper, and Father Blossom declared that he would drive fifty miles any day to get a slice of Linda's homemade bread.

"Mother, " whispered Meg, pulling her mother's sleeve half-way through the meal, "Dot's crying! "

Sure enough, Dot was crying, big, slow, salty tears running down her pink cheeks and dropping off into her bowl of rich milk and bread.

"Why darling! " said Mother Blossom in alarm. "Don't you feel well? Are you tired? Here, come sit in Mother's lap and tell her what the trouble is. "

Dot put down her spoon and ran to her mother, who lifted her up. The little girl buried her face in Mother Blossom's frilly collar and began to sob.

"P-oor Mr. Harley! " she choked. "We're having such a nice time, and he can't find his two little boys! I kn-ow he'd like to eat supper wif 'em! "

Dot seldom used "baby talk" but to-night she was tired and excited.

"Bless the child, what is she talking about? " demanded Aunt Polly curiously. "And look at this battery of solemn round eyes! What ever ails these lambs, Margaret? "

Mother Blossom, holding Dot close, explained about Mr. Harley.

"Didn't his wife stop here, Polly? " she asked. "Can you recall whether she said where she was going? Just a word might give him something definite to work on. "

Aunt Polly shook her head.

"I remember seeing her very well, " she said. "She had the two boys with her and I wanted her to spend the night. But no, she insisted she must 'go to the city'. Then I suggested that she leave the boys with me until she found work, if that was what she wanted, and that, I think, frightened her. I couldn't coax her to stay for supper after that. I certainly am sorry for Mr. Harley. Tell him his wife spoke most kindly of him and evidently believed that he was not in his right mind when he left her and the children. "

Twaddles being discovered asleep with a cake in one hand and a piece of bread and butter in the other, the four little Blossoms were swept away to hot baths and bed a few minutes after Aunt Polly finished. And the next thing they knew it was bright daylight and Jud was whistling on his way to the milking.

"I'm going, too! " Bobby hopped out of bed and began to dress hastily.

"So'm I! " Dot sat up and shook Meg. The troubles of Mr. Harley had fled with Dot's dreams and she was her usual merry self. "Come on, Meg, we haven't seen Carlotta yet. "

Meg was ready to get up and Twaddles woke before Bobby had tied one shoe, so the four little Blossoms, helping each other, managed to be dressed and downstairs before Jud had started to milk.

"Well, if this doesn't seem like old times! " he exclaimed grinning at them as they entered the barn.

"Forgotten how to milk, Meg? " asked Peter Apgar, coming into the dairy barn from feeding the horses. "Want to try it this morning? "

"I don't think I've forgotten how, " said Meg cautiously, "but I'd rather Jud milked, 'cause he can do it so much faster than I can; and then he can go round with us and see the things. "

That little speech pleased Jud mightily and pleased Peter Apgar, too, because, you will remember, Peter was Jud's father.

"You go sight-seeing this minute, Jud, " he ordered his tall son. "Guess I can do the milking on a special morning like this. "

So the four little Blossoms and Jud went to pay their respects to all the dear farm animals the children had known that first summer they spent on Brookside Farm. Carlotta, the calf given to Meg and Bobby, had grown to be a beautiful sleek cow and Meg privately decided she was prettier than any Aunt Polly owned. Jerry and Terry, the two farm horses, acted as though they remembered the small visitors; and as for Mrs. Sally Sweet, Aunt Polly's pet Jersey cow, she came right up to the bars and fairly begged to have her nose stroked.

"Mother will want to see you, " said Jud, when they had made the rounds of the barns and poultry yards.

Jud was "as nice as ever, " Meg said, and the winter he had spent at an agricultural college had given him more confidence in his own ability. He was as determined as ever, the children found, to be a farmer and a good one.

At Mrs. Peter's neat front door they found Mr. Tom Sparks, a man who sold and bought cattle and who had given Carlotta to Meg and Bobby. He was surprised and delighted to see the four children again and said it was just his usual good luck that had made him drive in that morning; he was going off the next morning on a two weeks' trip to buy cows.

"I'd almost like to live here, " confided Dot to Twaddles as they went in to breakfast.

CHAPTER IX

ON THE WAY AGAIN

Early the next morning Father Blossom brought the car around and, amid much hugging and kissing and a few tears, the good-bys were said. The Blossoms promised that if Aunt Polly and Linda and Jud did not get to see them while they were on Apple Tree Island, they would surely stop at Brookside Farm on their way home.

"I wonder how Mr. Harley feels now? " said Meg suddenly, when, the farm far behind, they were riding swiftly toward Sunset Lake. "I haven't thought about him all the time we were playing; have you, Dot? "

"No, I haven't, " admitted Dot. "But I'm sorry for him, just the same. Do you suppose he has found Mrs. Harley? "

"I'm afraid not, " answered Father Blossom.

"We will see him to-day, though, and give him what little news Aunt Polly could tell us of his wife. I am going to Greenpier, the little town where Chris Smith has his boats. I rather think Mr. Harley will bunk right there with him. Chris is a bachelor and will probably be glad to have some one live with him. "

Sunset Lake was twenty miles from Aunt Polly's farm, and the Blossoms arrived there before noon. There was no trouble in finding Chris Smith's boathouse, for Greenpier was a very small, shabby town and the large sign "Boats for Hire" was easily the most conspicuous thing in the place.

"Howdy! " Mr. Harley greeted them, shuffling over the road from the wharf as Father Blossom honked the horn and brought the car to a stop. "I'm just back from a trip to the island. Did you see your sister, Ma'am? "

Mother Blossom told Mr. Harley all that Aunt Polly knew of Mrs. Harley and all that she had said. He merely nodded his head. Meg noticed that while he had been neatly dressed when they overtook him on the road he now wore no tie and in place of a collar a rather grimy red handkerchief was knotted around his throat.

"I told you there wouldn't be a bridge, " whispered Twaddles to Dot. "Mother, all the way here Dot was arguing we went to the island on a bridge. We don't, do we? "

"I'm afraid you're so hungry you can't argue very pleasantly, " returned Mother Blossom. "However, I want you to wait till we get to the bungalow and I'll have a nice, hot lunch for you, Daddy, what about leaving the car? "

"There's a garage down the street a piece, " volunteered Mr. Harley. "Guess the car will be all right there; and the motor- boat's due any minute. "

"Told you there wasn't any bridge! " snickered Twaddles in triumph.

"Stop teasing your sister, " ordered Father Blossom. "Stay with Mother, children, till I run the car into the shop. Who runs the boat, Dick? "

"Man named Jenks, " answered Mr. Harley. "It makes two trips a day during the season; goes to all the islands and carries the mail and fresh vegetables. Jenks will do errands in town for you, too, if you want anything. Very obliging. Never gets mad. "

Mr. Harley spoke in short, jerky sentences that fascinated the listening children, Bobby especially.

"How many islands are there? " Meg wanted to know.

"'Bout eleven, " said Mr. Harley. "Some little, some big. Apple Tree Island? Oh, that's medium, I guess. "

Father Blossom came back from putting up the car and took charge of the suitcases. Each of the four little Blossoms carried his own coat. Presently they heard the chug-chug-chug of a motor-boat.

"All aboard! " called a bluff, hearty voice, and a green and white boat shot up beside the wharf on which the Blossoms stood.

"These passengers are for Apple Tree Island, " said Mr. Harley. "Know whether their baggage's come yet? "

"Poled three trunks and six small boxes over on the raft yesterday afternoon, " announced the motor-boat captain, who was also the crew. "Billed for the Winthrop bungalow—that right? "

"Right! " Father Blossom cheerfully assured him. "Now if you have room for us all, Captain—"

"Jenks, very much at your service, " said the captain, with a flourish. "I suppose you'd like to go right over? "

"We should, if you can take us, " said Mother Blossom. "The children are hungry and it must be after noon. "

Captain Jenks assured her that he could take them to Apple Tree Island without stopping at any other port, and as soon as they were comfortably on board he started his engine.

"Chug-chug-chug! " coughed the little motorboat.

It wasn't so little, of course, when it could carry seven passengers. Indeed it had a neat little forward deck and a tiny cabin upholstered in red leather that would be very cozy in bad weather. Captain Jenks thought his boat was a beauty. Bobby thought so, too.

"Like boats? " the captain asked him, finding the little boy at his elbow.

"I don't know much about them, " admitted Bobby. "Shall we have a boat like this? Daddy left the car in the garage. "

"A car's no good on the water, " said the captain loftily. "What you want is a seaworthy, tight little craft. You're going to live in the Winthrop bungalow, aren't you? Well, then, you'll have two rowboats. "

"Then Dot and I can have one, " Twaddles remarked with satisfaction.

Captain Jenks looked at him in some amazement.

"Wait till you try to lift an oar, " was his comment. "Hey, little girl, you'll get grease on your dress. "

"She has already, " said Meg calmly. "She always does. Are you named for the Captain Jenks in the rime? "

"Captain-Jenks-of-the-horse-marines-he-fed-his-horse-good-pork-and-beans? " inquired the captain glibly and in one breath. "Well, no, I don't think I was—not that I remember. One of the fellers that was up here last year made me a piece of poetry about my name. Want to hear it? "

The four little Blossoms nodded eagerly.

"Here 'tis, " said the captain. "Short and sweet:

> "Captain Jenks has a motor-boat,
> He feeds it oil to make it float. "

"What comes next? " demanded Dot.

"That's all, " said the captain. "And here we are at Apple Tree Island! "

"I hope you haven't been talked to death, " Father Blossom said to Captain Jenks when he came to tell the children it was time to get off. "My wife and I were trying to see if we could recognize the places we knew seven years ago. "

"Can't give me too many children, " said the captain heartily. "Any time you don't know what to do with these youngsters, you have 'em on the wharf when I tie up; I'll take 'em on my rounds with me and bring them back safely. "

CHAPTER X

ON THE ISLAND

There was a small wharf built out from a bank of green grass, and here the Blossoms landed, after bidding Captain Jenks a friendly good-by. They had been so busy talking to him, the children, that is, that they had never looked to see where the boat was taking them.

Apple Tree Island was only about half a mile from the shore, but perhaps a quarter of a mile further from Greenpier, where the stores and the post-office and the boathouse were built. A bend in the lake hid the island from the town. The ten or so other islands which Mr. Harley had mentioned were all further up the lake.

Mr. Harley had been mistaken in his estimation of the size of Apple Tree Island. It was in reality one of the smallest and, Father Blossom thought, less than two miles around its shoreline. It was diamond shaped, and the Winthrop bungalow was now the only building on it. Mr. Harley's shack no longer counted, and the summer home of the invalid for whom Father Blossom made yearly trips to the island, had burned to the ground during the winter. So the Blossoms would be the only people on the island this year.

"Just like Swiss Family Robinson! " exclaimed Meg rapturously. "Look at the funny stumpy trees! "

"We'll take a walk this afternoon and explore, " her mother promised. "Who is hungry enough to help me get lunch? "

They all were, it seemed, so they followed the worn path that led through a grassy field to the Winthrop bungalow. This house was so surrounded by trees that it could hardly be seen till one reached the front door, though from the porch glimpses of the lake could be had through the trees.

"What a perfectly darling house! " Meg exclaimed when she saw it.

Mr. Winthrop had built his house of gray fieldstone, and it was truly charming. There was a deep porch around three sides, a huge fireplace in the hall that also served as a living-room, and latticed windows in every room. Mrs. Winthrop had furnished the place in exquisite taste, and Mother Blossom declared that she could be happy all Summer if she never went out of the house.

She had found an apron in her bag and was busy scrambling eggs when she said that. Meg was setting the table in the kitchen, for one half of the room was designed to be used as the dining-room, and Dot and Twaddles were filling the salt cellars amiably. Father Blossom had lighted the oil stove, and Bobby was unpacking the plates. They had found all the things shipped from the Oak Hill home neatly stacked in the hall, ready to be opened.

"But you are going out of the house, " said Father Blossom decidedly. "This isn't going to be the kind of vacation where every one has a good time except Mother. With five pairs of hands to help you, don't you think you can manage to go with us on tramps and picnics? And you used to like to row. "

"I do yet, " replied Mother Blossom. "Of course, if you all help me, I'll play when you play. But lunch is ready, children. Dot, what have you done to the front of that frock? "

"I shut it in the bathroom door, " explained Dot. "It's only ripped a little. "

She had torn it clear of the yoke so that it hung below her petticoat bodice, but every one was too excited and hungry to pay much attention to a torn frock.

After lunch, first washing the dishes, the Blossoms decided to try to walk around the island. Unpacking, said Mother Blossom, could be done as well in the morning.

It was a clear, cool day; indeed, the Blossoms soon found that it was rare when a breeze did not sweep steadily over Apple Tree Island. And, as Twaddles wrote to Norah, they "used blankets every night."

The Blossoms discovered that Apple Tree Island gained its name from the fact that at each of its four points grew a sturdy, flourishing apple tree. These were the only apple trees on the island, though there were a number of other kinds, the majority of them curiously shaped and stunted. There were rocks on one side of the island, but on the other the shore sloped down to the lake gradually and was covered with grass almost to the water's edge. There was a gravelly beach tucked away between two points, and Bobby immediately wished for his bathing suit. But he agreed to wait till morning for his first swim.

"Look at that funny heap of stones ahead, " said Meg, as they rounded the point of the island farthest from the bungalow. "Look, you can see where the chimney was! "

"And there's a broken express wagon, " added Dot. "Do you suppose a little boy used to live there? "

Father Blossom gave a low whistle of surprise.

"Children, " he announced gravely, "that is where the Harleys used to live. " Then to Mother Blossom: "It has fallen to pieces since I was up here last Summer. I think part of it was struck by lightning. "

CHAPTER XI

A DAMP ADVENTURE

The Harley shack had never been a very fine building, but it had once been a home and, though the four little Blossoms were too small to realize it, it was the sight of the forlorn chimney and fireplace, the broken express wagon and the broken bits of furniture that made them feel sad.

"Why do I want to cry, Mother? " Meg kept asking. "What makes me sorry? "

"'Cause we don't know where Mrs. Harley went, " asserted Twaddles wisely.

"That's it, darling, " said Mother Blossom tenderly.

From the Harley shack, the Blossoms went down to the shore and, by using Father Blossom's field glasses, were able to see the two islands that lay to the north of Apple Tree Island and which, rumor said, were used by smugglers. But the children could not forget the Harleys, and as they continued their walk around the island they discussed the mysterious disappearance of Mrs. Harley and the children.

"I wish we could find 'em! " said Meg earnestly. "Wouldn't that be fine, Bobby? "

"Yes. But how can we? " replied the practical Bobby. "They aren't on the island, and we are. Perhaps they went to China. "

"I'm so sorry for Mr. Harley, " struck in Dot. "Do you remember his little boys, Bobby? "

Bobby wasn't sure.

"I don't think I do, " he answered cautiously. "If one of 'em wore a blue sailor suit with a red tie and the other had long pants, then I do; I'll ask Mother. "

"My dear little son! " exclaimed Mother Blossom, laughing when Bobby asked her if the Harley boys wore such clothes. "They were little fellows, about the size of Twaddles—how could one of them wear long trousers? And you were eight months old, just a little baby. You are thinking of some other boys you have seen. "

Because Father Blossom had insisted that Mother Blossom was to enjoy a real vacation, there was very little unpacking to be done. The Winthrops had left their bungalow fully furnished, and though there was no one on the island to help with the housework, Mother Blossom declared that if they all helped her there would not be much to do. In a few days they felt very much at home and the children voted Apple Tree Island quite as delightful as Brookside Farm.

"Where you going, Dot? " Twaddles called one morning soon after they had arrived.

"I was going to look for you, " said Dot importantly. "We're all going over on the ten o'clock boat—Captain Jenks' boat, you know. Mother has some letters to mail, and she wants us to take the wash over, that is if Captain Jenks knows any one in Greenpier who will wash and iron dresses. Meg and Bobby are down on the wharf with the basket now. "

"Well, well, how are all my friends? " Captain Jenks greeted them when his boat came chugging up to the wharf and he saw a patient row of small people waiting to go on board. "Want to come now, or shall I stop on the return trip? "

"We'd like to sail back with you, " aid Bobby. "Mother thought you didn't go any farther up. "

"Special trip this morning, " answered the captain. "Have to stop at the island north of Harley's shack to see if any one's violating game laws. I'm a little of everything 'round here— sheriff and warden and lake captain. You can come, and welcome. "

"We have to take care of the twins, " Bobby informed him as the four little Blossoms marched aboard over the gangplank Captain Jenks let down especially for them. "Meg and I are old enough to go to town but Dot and Twaddles are only four. "

"What is in the basket? " asked the kind captain, fearing an explosion from Twaddles, who was furious at this public reference to his age.

"Oh, that's the wash! " said Bobby. "Mother wants to know if any one in Greenpier will wash and iron clothes? "

"Four of you going specially on that errand, I suppose, " chuckled the captain, "and not one of you remembered what you were going for. Sure I know some one who will wash 'em and iron 'em up in great style and be glad of the job. Mrs. Clayton's her name. Here, Bobby, you don't have to get off—I'll catch that basket. "

Captain Jenks took a long pole with a hook on one end of it that he used to hook fruit baskets and crates and bundles with, and neatly drew the clothes basket on board. Mother Blossom had tied the clothes in securely and put paper over the top, knowing, perhaps, that the basket was destined to have an adventurous journey.

"Are there smugglers on the island? " Bobby asked the captain, as the motor-boat churned up the water swiftly, and they left Apple Tree Island behind.

"Well, no, I wouldn't say that, " replied the captain. "But we've had it reported that people living in Reville, that's a town up Sunset Lake almost opposite Kidd's Island where we're going, have seen fires on the beach at night. It's closed season now for the birds, and if any one is shooting 'em, we want to know it. "

"Are you a policeman? " asked Twaddles in awe.

"Something like it, " admitted the captain. "Leastways, I'm a deputy sheriff. Pretty place, isn't it? "

The boat was approaching the island, and it was indeed a pretty place. It was smaller than Apple Tree Island and had fewer trees, but it was completely covered with thick green grass brightly starred over with daisies. And not a single daisy grew on Apple Tree Island!

"Oh, oh, oh! " cried Meg softly. "How lovely! See, Dot, millions and millions of daisies. "

"You can pick some while I take a look around, " said Captain Jenks, fastening the boat with an iron chain and hook to a ring sunk in a wooden post. There was no wharf because no one lived on the island to build one and very few boats came there anyway.

Bobby and Twaddles stuck close to the captain's heels, but Meg and Dot determined to get some daisies to take home to their mother. They worked busily, and by the time the others were back from their inspection of the little open shed which was the only shelter on the island, the two girls had large bouquets.

"Were there any smugglers? " asked Dot half-fearfully.

"That's a silly story, that smuggler stuff, " pronounced Captain Jenks. "To my mind a man who breaks the game laws is worse than a smuggler. We found the ashes of his campfire and this. " He held up a pair of bird wings.

"The poor little bird! " exclaimed Meg compassionately. "How can any one shoot a bird! "

"It's all right sometimes, isn't it? " Bobby insisted. "Jud goes gunning, Meg, you know he does. "

"I've nothing to say against it when the season is open, " said the captain.

Captain Jenks seemed saddened by the discovery of the pretty, spotted wings, but when he had put them away in a little box in the cabin he cheered up and admired the daisies.

"You'll find string in that toolchest, " he directed them. "Going to make two bunches? That's right—I don't like to see flowers crowded even after they're picked. "

The two bunches were tied to the rail as a safe place and one in which they would not be easily crushed. The motor-boat—by the way, its name was The Sarah, painted in green letters; you haven't been told that before, have you? —was now chugging down the lake toward Greenpier, and Bobby and Meg were taking their first lesson in managing the wheel. Twaddles had found a compass in the toolchest and was having a wonderful time playing with that. Dot thought the time had come to put an idea of hers into practice.

"They look wilted, " she told herself, eyeing the daisies with disfavor. "What they need is water. "

So this mischievous child took a long string and tied it to each bunch of daisies; then she held it in the middle and allowed them to trail in the water.

The Sarah was almost at Greenpier before Meg glanced toward Dot and saw what she was doing.

"Dot Blossom! " she cried, rushing toward her. "You'll spoil 'em. Oh, Bobby, look what Dot's doing to the daisies! "

In her anxiety to get the daisies wet, Dot had climbed to the top of the rail, and when Meg shouted at her so suddenly she was startled. She tried to catch the rail, missed it, and tumbled into the water.

Dear, dear, there was a hubbub, you may be sure. Luckily the boat was in very shallow water and a man sitting on the wharf jumped in and had Dot in his arms almost as soon as she splashed. He was Mr. Harley and he easily walked ashore. The water was only as high as his waist.

"You're not drowned, " he kept telling Dot, who was sadly frightened and crying bitterly. "You're only wet, Sister. "

"Take her up to Mrs. Clayton's, " ordered Captain Jenks. "We were headed for there, and she always has a big fire on account of the ironing. She'll know what to do. "

Apparently Mr. Harley knew where Mrs. Clayton lived, for he strode away with Dot in his arms. Captain Jenks, Meg and Bobby and Twaddles had to run to keep up with him. He stopped before a whitewashed cottage with a woman ironing in the large front room.

"Can you dry this baby off and give her something hot to drink? " asked Captain Jenks, and Mrs. Clayton held out her arms for Dot.

The little girl was indignant at being called "baby" but her teeth were chattering from cold and fright, and the hot cocoa Mrs. Clayton presently gave her tasted very good. She went off to sleep after that, wrapped in a warm blanket, and woke to find her clothes dry and ironed.

Mrs. Clayton was a stout, comfortable, jolly kind of woman who did washing and ironing for the Summer people on the various islands and in the shore towns that bordered Sunset Lake. She promised to have Mother Blossom's clothes ready a week from that day, and the children trotted back to the boat, Dot none the worse for her experience. They knew no one at home would be worried, though Dot had slept two hours, because they were not expected back till the afternoon boat.

"We had cocoa and jelly sandwiches while you were asleep, " Twaddles informed his sister. "And Mrs. Clayton has a ship carved out of a piece of bone! "

At the wharf they found Mr. Harley and Chris Smith, the boathouse man, and Captain Jenks, all very glad to see them and glad that Dot's ducking had not been worse. The captain had several other passengers to another island on this trip.

"I'll be over in a day or two, " said Mr. Harley, as the children boarded The Sarah. "Might as well look around the place once in a while. "

Father Blossom was waiting on their wharf when they reached Apple Tree Island, and his first question was whether they had found some one to do the washing to save Mother Blossom from attempting too much.

"Yes, and she's already started, " cried Bobby eagerly. "She washed and ironed Dot! "

CHAPTER XII

SUNNY SUMMER DAYS

"Washed and ironed Dot! " repeated Father Blossom. "Why, what happened to Dot? "

The four little Blossoms explained, and then they had to tell the story again to Mother Blossom when they went up to the bungalow. Father and Mother Blossom were so glad and so grateful that the accident had turned out so fortunately, when it might easily have had serious consequences, that they scolded no one. Dot was sure that she would not climb up on the rail of The Sarah another time, and Father and Mother Blossom knew she would be careful.

Such fun as the children had in the days that followed! Mother Blossom declared that they almost lived in their bathing suits, and indeed, as the warm weather came on, a bathing suit for the sunny hours of the morning was the most comfortable costume any one could hope for. The little bathing beach was not too far from the bungalow, and Father Blossom was an excellent swimmer. He taught each child to swim and very cunning Twaddles and Dot looked in the water. Dot wore a scarlet bathing cap on her dark hair and her bathing suit was red, too, while Twaddles wore a navy and white suit. Meg's suit was a lighter blue and her cap was white, and Bobby had a brown suit like Father Blossom's. The children thought that no one could look lovelier than their mother in her black and white suit and cap to match, and indeed Mother Blossom was growing prettier every day. She said she had not had a real vacation in so long that she felt as the children did—as if she must play outdoors every minute.

Sometimes they took their supper down to the beach and Father Blossom and Bobby built a fire and they had toasted bread and bacon; sometimes they went hunting for beach plums, that odd fruit that grows on tall bushes and which make such delicious jam; sometimes they all went fishing in the two rowboats, Mother Blossom rowing one and Father Blossom the other.

"I caught the biggest fish, " Dot wrote to Norah, "only it wasn't a fish—it was somebody's old boot. "

But Twaddles and Meg, oddly enough, had the best luck of any of the fishermen. Meg rarely went fishing that she did not bring home a nice little string of fish she had caught herself (though Bobby had to bait her hooks), and as for Twaddles, he never paid much attention to his line except to pull it in now and then to take a fish off. One day the whim seized him to fish from the wharf, and when Bobby was sent to call him to supper Twaddles calmly showed him four fine fish he had caught in less than an hour.

"I'll take you on a fishing trip some day for a mascot, " said Captain Jenks, who continued to be a very good friend.

The four little Blossoms had gone over with him on The Sarah the week after Dot's adventure in the water to get the wash from Mrs. Clayton. Bobby and Meg had been a little fearful that Mother Blossom would not trust them again to take care of the twins, but that dear lady knew that accidents make wise little folk more careful. She assured Bobby and Meg with a kiss that she was sure they would look after Dot and Twaddles more closely this time. They did; indeed, the twins rather resented the strict supervision under which they made the trip to Greenpier, but when Dot appealed to Captain Jenks, to her disappointment, he sided with Bobby and Meg.

"I have an uneasy feelin' that I don't know what you might take into your head to do next, " the captain told the surprised little girl. "If I was your sister and brother, I'd tie a string to you and then I'd know where you were every minute. "

However, of all their games and pastimes, the one of which the four little Blossoms never tired, was to go and play around the ruins of the Harley shack. The island was so safe a place, such an ideal playground for little people, that Father and Mother Blossom felt no uneasiness no matter where the children went. They must be home punctually to meals and they must not go in the water anywhere without asking permission and then only on the bathing beach if no older person was with them. These few rules were all they had to remember and it was small wonder that they often said Apple Tree Island was the nicest place in the world! Aunt Polly had sent Bobby a little watch and he could "tell time" nicely; so no matter how far they wandered they had no excuse for not coming back to the bungalow when Mother Blossom set them a time limit.

"Let's go to Mr. Harley's house, " suggested Meg one bright morning.

That was the way they always spoke of the forlorn shack—it was "Mr. Harley's house. "

"All right, let's, " agreed Bobby. "I'll ask Mother if we can take our lunch. We don't want the twins this time, do we? "

Bobby and Meg had been washing the breakfast dishes while Mother Blossom, at the pretty desk in the large hall, was making out a grocery list for Father Blossom to take to town on the morning boat. Meg and Bobby were learning to be the best little helpers one ever saw; in fact, this Summer all the children had learned a great deal about housekeeping and they meant to astonish Norah with their knowledge when they went home.

"I think it would be nice if we could play by ourselves, " said Meg gently, in answer to Bobby's question.

Meg and Bobby sometimes felt that they would like to play a game without the aid of Dot and Twaddles. Not that they did not love the small sister and brother dearly, but Meg and Bobby usually liked to do the very same thing in the very same way, and Dot and Twaddles were apt to want to do it six different ways and all at once! That, as you may understand, occasionally led to disputes.

"Take your lunch and play at Mr. Harley's house? " said Mother Blossom, laying down her pencil and smiling at the two earnest faces. "I don't know why not. I'll put some sandwiches up for you as soon as I finish this list. "

"And may just Meg and I go, Mother? " added Bobby coaxingly.

"Oh, Bobby, you know the twins will be disappointed, " Mother Blossom replied. "They do love to poke around that shack and I'm afraid they will feel hurt if they think you do not want them. "

She tapped her pencil absently on the desk for a moment.

"I tell you, children, " she cried, putting an arm around each. "Suppose you and Meg, Bobby, go on to the shack and play by yourselves this morning; then, at noon, I'll send the twins with lunch for all of you and you stay an hour or two longer and play with them. How will that be? "

Meg and Bobby thought this was a splendid plan, and, only stopping to kiss Mother Blossom and to take an old rusty shovel which was Bobby's chief treasure, they ran off. Dot and Twaddles were down at the wharf waiting to see Captain Jenks and his motor-boat, a daily habit which was encouraged by the captain, who usually brought them some little treat.

"We'll go around the other side of the island, and they won't see us, " said Meg, the general. "It isn't much longer, really. "

The other side of the island was rockier, though, and the bushes were thicker. Still, Meg and Bobby managed to scramble though, and half an hour's steady tramping brought them to the Harley shack.

"It keeps falling apart, " mourned Meg; and indeed the place looked worse every time they visited it.

"Apples! " shouted Bobby, running forward to look under the gnarled trees. "Apples, Meg! Big ones! "

"They're not ripe, " said Meg promptly. "'Sides, they're not ours— they belong to Mr. Harley. Daddy says everything here belongs to him. "

"I guess they are green, " admitted Bobby, who had tried in vain to soften one in his fingers. "But apples belong to anybody, Meg. "

"They do not! " contradicted Meg. "Why, Bobby Blossom! how can you talk like that? Don't you remember when you and Twaddles were in the fruit store with Daddy last Spring and Twaddles took a strawberry from one of the boxes because he saw another boy do it? You know Daddy made him put it back before he could eat it. If strawberries don't belong to anybody, I guess apples don't. "

Meg's honest blue eyes looked beseechingly at her brother.

"All right, " surrendered Bobby. "I wasn't going to eat 'em, anyway. "

"I hope not, " said Meg severely. "What'll we play? "

"Hunting for treasure, " responded Bobby. "That's why I brought the shovel. You want to pound first? "

Meg and Bobby had invented this game. They pretended that hundreds of years ago fierce pirates had buried chests of gold and jewels on this end of the island and that the Harley shack had been the castle home of these wicked sea rovers. The pirates had died without leaving directions to tell where they had buried the treasure, and gradually the castle had crumbled away.

Then, one day, there came two brave sailors (some people called them Meg and Bobby) and they set to work to dig up the great iron chests. They meant to divide the money and jewels with the descendants of those from whom the pirates had stolen it. And their method of locating the buried treasure was to go about with a shovel and tap here and there. Where the earth gave out a hollow sound, there they would dig. These two sailors had not yet found anything, but it was certainly an exciting game.

"Dig here, Bobby! " cried Meg, when she had rapped the earth around the crazy chimney and persuaded herself that it sounded "hollow. "

So Bobby dug. And presently his shovel struck something.

"Oh, Bobby, what is it? " shrieked Meg. "Is it an iron chest? "

She really half-believed that Bobby had found the pirate's buried treasure.

The twins were scrambling over the rocks and they heard Meg's cry. Mother Blossom had kept them as long as she could, but they had insisted on setting out a half hour before noon and they had run most of the way, the lunch basket bumping wildly in time to their steps. Their faces red from the heat and streaming with perspiration, they burst into the ruins of the Harley house just as Bobby brushed the dirt from his find. "I don't know what it is, " said Bobby, trying to look closely at the odd-shaped little thing in his hand, with three children insisting on seeing it at the same time. "Look out, Dot, you nearly made me drop it. "

None of the children could guess what it was Bobby had found, and finally he slipped it into his pocket to take home and show Father Blossom. Then he discovered that he was hungry, and the twins proudly produced the basket.

"Have to wash first, " announced Bobby firmly. "Did you bring a towel? "

Mother Blossom had sent a towel, and Bobby pulled up a brimming bucket of water from the Harley well and poured the old tin wash basin full. The well had been thoroughly cleaned out that Spring by the men whom the Winthrops sent up to put the bungalow in order. They had wisely decided that it was better to have all the water on the island fit to drink rather than to try to keep any one from using an abandoned well.

"You and Dot wash, " commanded Bobby, when his face was washed and dried and his hands as neat as could be.

"I did wash my face 'fore breakfast, " insisted Twaddles indignantly. He thought that should last him a long time.

Bobby, however, was equally insistent, and Dot and Twaddles had to bathe their hands and faces before he would let them share in the contents of the lunch basket. Mother Blossom was used to satisfying four good appetites, and the children ate every crumb she had sent them.

Then they went back to their game, and Twaddles and Dot tried their luck at locating buried treasure.

"Dig here, Bobby! " Twaddles cried. "This place sounds hollow, honest it does. "

"You don't tell me! " said another voice, a man's voice. "Why do you suppose that is? "

Twaddles jumped, and Meg turned around, startled.

CHAPTER XIII

A SIGNAL FOR HELP

"Didn't scare you, did I? " said Mr. Harley, walking into the circle and smiling at the perplexed faces.

"We didn't hear you coming, " answered Bobby. "Did you row over?"

"Yes, I came over to tell your mother that your father couldn't get back till the afternoon boat, " Mr. Harley explained. "Your mother wanted to know if I'd come and fetch you. "

"Does she want us? " asked Meg quickly. "Oh! What was that? "

"Thunder, " answered Mr. Harley, shortly. "Your mother sent you two umbrellas, but I don't think we'd better start now; the storm is 'most ready to break. Guess you were having such a good time you never heard the rumbling. "

It was true. The children had never glanced up, or they would have seen the great white clouds that, mounting higher and higher, gradually darkened and then shut out the sun. They would have heard the angry mutterings of thunder and seen the sharp streaks of lightning, but the game of hunting for treasure had completely absorbed them.

"It will rain on us, " remarked Meg nervously. "There isn't any roof, you know. "

Then she blushed. She wondered if Mr. Harley thought they were selfish to amuse themselves in his tumble-down home, and whether it was polite of her to mention that the roof was gone.

"We'll have to make a roof, " said Mr. Harley capably. "Let's see; if we take that door and put it across these two barrels, that will keep the rain off. Here's a piece of oilcloth we can use for a curtain to shut the lightning out. Now we're as comfy as we would be in a regular house. "

While he spoke, he had lifted what had once been the front door of his house, placed it across two barrels and draped across the open side a large square of oilcloth that was cracked and creased in many places but still waterproof. The barrels were against the one wall of the house left standing, so that, when all was fixed, the small shelter was fairly comfortable.

Bobby, feeling in his pocket for a nail to pin the oilcloth more securely, touched the queer object his shovel had unearthed that morning.

"Look what I found, " he said eagerly, holding out the little pointed specimen.

"Arrow head, " said Mr. Harley. "Indians once lived on this island, and you're likely to turn those things up most anywhere. Will your mother be afraid alone in the bungalow? "

"Mother's never afraid, " declared Bobby confidently, putting the arrow head back in his pocket to show his father. "Oh, that lightning went right into the lake! "

"Better get in now, " Mr. Harley told them, holding up the oilcloth so that they could creep in under the door-roof. "All in? Then here I come. "

The rain was coming down in great, dashing torrents in another moment and the four little Blossoms were thankful for their dry corner.

"It's a good thing we didn't start out, " shouted Mr. Harley above the noise of the rain. "We never could have made the bungalow before the rain caught us. This will knock the apples off. That's a pity because they're fine when they're left to ripen. "

"Meg said they weren't ripe yet, " said Bobby.

"I hope you didn't try to eat any, " answered Mr. Harley earnestly. "Green apples are not good for you. "

"Oh, we didn't touch one, " Bobby assured him, trying to punch Twaddles, who was tickling him. "Meg said they belonged to you. "

"I want you children to eat 'em, but not till they are ripe, " Mr. Harley shouted back. "Along about the first week in July, you come up here and you'll find the best sweet apples you ever tasted. That is, if the storms leave any on the tree, and I guess they will. You eat all you want—I never want to taste one of those apples again! "

Twaddles stopped trying to tickle Bobby, and Meg squeezed Dot's hand excitedly. Poor Mr. Harley!

"Then—then you haven't heard about your little boys? " asked Bobby hesitatingly.

"Not a word, " groaned Mr. Harley. "It's as though the earth had opened and swallowed 'em. I can't, for the life of me, figure out where they could have gone. Sometimes I get to thinking they're here, and I can't rest till I get a boat and row over. One night I got up at one o'clock and rowed here; but Lou and the boys were just as far away as ever. "

The rain was coming more gently now, and the heaviest clouds had passed over the island. Mr. Harley lifted the oilcloth flap, and the four little Blossoms felt a refreshing breeze sweep in upon them.

"We can start in a minute or so, " announced Mr. Harley, opening the umbrellas.

A few minutes later they started in a fine drizzle of rain. That, however, soon stopped and the sun came out, and by the time they had reached the bungalow, to find Father Blossom just coming up from the wharf and Mother Blossom, not a bit frightened by the storm, on the porch, the only trace of the thunderstorm was the wet grass and the dripping eaves of the pretty bungalow.

May swept into June and June was nearly gone when one morning Father Blossom announced that he wanted to take Mother Blossom over to Greenpier in the rowboat and that he hoped the children could persuade her that they would be all right if left to themselves for a little while.

"I don't think we'll be gone more than two or three hours, " said Father Blossom seriously; "and while I don't suppose this day means anything to you, it does mean a good deal to Mother and to me. And if you children will take care of each other, we'll be back before you have time to miss us. "

"I know what day it is, " Meg cried proudly. "It's the day you and Mother were married! "

She remembered from the last June, and Mother Blossom had not thought any of the children would remember.

"I do hope they will be all right, Ralph, " she said a little anxiously, as Father Blossom handed her into the rowboat and took the oars and the four little Blossoms stood on the wharf and waved to them.

"Of course they will be all right, " Father Blossom asserted sturdily.

"Daddy, oh, Daddy! " called Bobby after the boat, "may we have your field glasses? "

"All right, only be careful of them, " Father Blossom called back.

"What'll we do? " asked Dot, as they left the wharf and walked back to the bungalow.

"Go up to the Harley house and see if we can see the pirates' haunted ships, " answered Bobby. "We can look 'way off with the glasses. Where 'bouts are they, Meg? "

"I know. I'll get 'em, " said Meg eagerly.

She ran upstairs and found the glasses hanging on the wall in their leather case. They were a very fine pair, and the children were not often allowed to use them.

The "haunted ships" that Bobby spoke of, were another "pretend" the children enjoyed. Mother Blossom, reading to them one night, had found a poem that told how the ships of the pirates were condemned forever to sail the seas. The poem went on to say that sometimes people saw these ghostly ships and that when they did some of the buried treasure, part of the ill-gotten gains they had once carried on their decks, was sure to be unearthed.

"I can't see a single ship, " reported Bobby, when, after the four children had walked to the north end of the island, he adjusted the glasses and took a long look.

"Let me try, " begged Meg.

She stared so long that Twaddles grew impatient for his turn.

"Hurry up, Meg, " he urged. "I want to see. Bobby, can't I have 'em now? "

"Don't bother me, " said Meg impatiently. "I see something. Look, Bobby, isn't that something moving on Kidd's island? "

"Let me look, Meg. Why, it's somebody waving a rag tied on a pole."

Sure enough, it was. Neither Bobby nor Meg could make out what it was that held the pole, but it certainly was a pole with a bit of cloth dipping crazily about from one end of it.

"Isn't that funny? " puzzled Meg, staring at Bobby. "No one lives on Kidd's Island. "

Dot's mind was full of pirates; and no wonder, for the four children had talked and played pirate games for weeks.

"I'll bet a pirate is there and he wants you to come so he can kidnap you, " said Dot solemnly.

Twaddles was staring through the glasses, his "turn" having come at last.

"Maybe he's a sick pirate, " he ventured.

"Meg, " said Bobby suddenly, "I'll bet that's a signal for help; or if it isn't, some one ought to go to see what it is. It's almost time for Captain Jenks—let's run down to the wharf and tell him. "

It lacked ten minutes of the time the captain's boat was due, and the four little Blossoms started pell-mell on a run for the wharf. Meg carried the glasses, remembering even in her hurry that they had promised to take care of them.

"Captain Jenks! Oh, Captain Jenks! " cried Bobby, hailing the skipper of The Sarah before it had even begun to turn toward the shore.

"Oh, Captain Jenks! " quavered Meg.

"Captain Jenks! " squeaked Dot. "Listen, Captain Jenks! "

"What do you suppose—" began Twaddles as The Sarah grated against the wharf and Captain Jenks surveyed the waving arms brandished before him.

"House afire? " asked the captain placidly.

"Oh, no! " sputtered Bobby, the words tumbling over each other. "Nothing like that! But there's somebody on Kidd's Island! "

"There is? " said the captain sharply. "How do you know? "

Meg and Bobby and Dot and Twaddles insisted on all explaining at once, but somehow the captain succeeded in understanding what they were trying to tell him.

"Waving a rag, eh? " he said thoughtfully. "Well, I might take a little run up there, though I wasn't calculating to go so far north this morning.

"May we go? Please, may we go? " pleaded Bobby.

"Ask your mother—or no, give me the glasses, and I'll have a squint at this waving rag, " answered the captain. "Maybe it won't be anything you'll want to see. "

He took the glasses from Meg and strode off to the Harley shack, followed by the children, who were now almost beside themselves with excitement.

Captain Jenks took a long look toward Kidd's Island, then whistled.

"Well, I never! " he said softly, as though speaking to himself.

"What is it? " asked Bobby. "May we go? "

"I guess it will be all right, Son, " replied the captain kindly. "Run ask your mother, and if she is willing, I'll take you all. "

"Mother isn't at home, " explained Bobby. "She and Daddy rowed to Greenpier. She would say yes, I know she would. "

"Well—all right! " decided Captain Jenks. "I'll take you to Kidd's Island and drop you here at the wharf on the way back. I think we're going to be what the papers call a rescuing party. "

The four little Blossoms hurried on board The Sarah before the captain should change his mind. A rescue! Could anything be more exciting! As Twaddles remarked afterward, he wouldn't have missed coming to Apple Tree Island for anything in the world.

The captain took the wheel, and the boat chug-chugged swiftly toward Kidd's Island. When they were off shore they could see the rag quite plainly. It was a small handkerchief tied to an oar.

But no pirate was waving the forlorn little signal.

"Look, look! " cried Meg, as though afraid Captain Jenks might not see. "It's a girl and two little boys! "

CHAPTER XIV

THE RESCUE

The four little Blossoms crowded to the rail of The Sarah and stared dumbly at the slim girl in a pink frock who had been waving the oar.

"Why, if it isn't Letty Blake! " said Captain Jenks cheerfully. "How long have you been living on Kidd's Island? "

To the surprise of the children, Letty Blake flung her oar to one side and sat down in the sand and cried.

Captain Jenks hastily tied his boat to the wooden post and jumped ashore.

"You're all right now, child, " he told the girl, patting her kindly on the shoulder. "Look at all the crew who offered to come help me rescue you. And who are these small tykes? "

The two little boys came closer to Letty. "They're my cousins, " explained Letty, drying her eyes. "They came to visit us last week; and I took them for a row this morning and we wanted to get some flowers. I thought I tied the boat, but when we looked up it was drifting off. Oh, dear! "

"There, there, " said Captain Jenks comfortably. "Nothing to cry about, Letty. Lots of people find out too late they didn't fasten the boat. Hop ashore, youngsters, and I'll introduce you to new friends."

The four little Blossoms, though bursting with curiosity, had remained politely on deck. Now at Captain Jenk's invitation, they joined hands and jumped, landing like four plump little ducks.

"Letty, " declared the captain gravely, "here are four mighty good friends of mine, Meg and Bobby and Dot and Twaddles Blossom. They don't use any other names in the summer time. "

The four little Blossoms giggled at this and Letty Blake smiled a little. She was a pretty girl, apparently about twelve years old, with dark blue eyes and a tanned skin that showed she was used to outdoor living.

"These are my cousins, Nelson and Albert Bennett, " she said, pulling the two boys forward.

"Hello! " beamed Twaddles, who seldom suffered from shyness. "We came to rescue you. "

"Don't want to be rescued, " said Nelson suddenly. "Do we, Letty? "

"Of course we do, " retorted his cousin. "How do you expect to get any lunch if we have to stay on this island? And where would you sleep? We're going on board The Sarah this minute and Captain Jenks will take us home. "

Letty had stopped crying, and now she shouldered the oar, ready to carry it to The Sarah.

"How's it come you have one oar? " asked Captain Jenks, plainly puzzled. "Where's the other? "

"In the boat, " said Letty. "We brought this ashore because the boys wanted to play jungle travelers and carry things slung on a pole over their shoulders. But the oar was too heavy for them to lift. "

Captain Jenks laughed as he marshaled the children on the boat.

"I suppose Uncle Silas will be put out over the boat being lost, " said Letty thoughtfully, pulling Nelson and Albert out of the captain's way as he started the engine. "He had just painted it and the oarlocks were new this year. I wish I had made sure that knot was tied. "

"No use grieving over what's done and past, " said Captain Jenks wisely. "Meg, we're going to lose Dot overboard again, if she isn't removed from that railing. "

Sure enough, there was Dot half way over the railing, her small sandals hooked around a cleat in an endeavor to keep her balance. Just as Meg opened her mouth to call her, she turned.

"Ship ahoy! " she cried, trying to imitate Captain Jenk's most nautical term.

"Starboard or port? " asked the captain gravely, though his eyes twinkled.

The four little Blossoms had picked up several odds and ends of navigation in the few weeks they had known the captain, but Dot was too excited to remember what she had learned.

"It's right HERE" she shouted. "Oh, you'll run into it! "

"The rowboat! The rowboat! " cried Letty, dancing up and down. "Oh, Captain Jenks, what do you think of that? It's Uncle Silas's boat and the oar is in it, and our sweaters and everything! "

"Fine! But don't lose your heads, " said Captain Jenks placidly. No one had ever seen him agitated. "Bobby, you take the wheel and hold it steady. "

Bobby proudly took the wheel, and Captain Jenks, while the others watched breathlessly, brought the rowboat alongside with a long iron hook and with another drew up the long rope that was tied to an iron ring in the prow.

Then the rowboat was fastened to the stern of The Sarah, and, as Captain Jenks remarked, the rescue was complete.

Soon they reached the wharf on Apple Tree Island, and the four little Blossoms were put ashore, after saying good-by to Letty Blake and her cousins. She lived in Greenpier, and Captain Jenks had known her since she was Dot's age.

"Let's have lunch ready by the time Daddy and Mother come back, " suggested Meg. "We can do it every bit ourselves. "

Working like four beavers, they soon had lunch—and a good lunch, too—set out on the table. They had promised never to light the oil stove, so they could not make tea, but Mother Blossom could do that in a very few minutes when she came.

When the table was ready Meg ran out for some red clover and tall grasses for a bouquet and Bobby followed her, leaving Dot and Twaddles alone.

"I think we ought to have some jelly on the table, don't you? " said Dot. "We never have enough jelly. Mother likes currant. "

"You get it, and I'll open it, " promised Twaddles. "Bobby never lets me have the can opener. "

Dot got a chair and climbed up on it. She was just able to reach the shelf in the closet where the tumblers of jelly were kept. She knew that currant jelly was red and she handed down a ruby red glass to the waiting Twaddles.

"Don't cut yourself, " she admonished him as he punched the can opener into the tin lid.

Twaddles and Dot did not know that jelly tumblers are not opened with can openers. Mother Blossom and Norah always pried off the tin lids and used them the next year for other glasses.

"Oh, gee, there's a lot of wax on top, " Twaddles reported when he had torn a jagged hole in the lid and found the jelly was protected with a layer of paraffin. "How'll I get that off? "

"Take a fork, " advised Dot. "Here—I'll show you. "

She seized a fork and jammed it into the paraffin. Bits of wax and jelly flew from the glass, splashing Twaddles' clean blouse and plentifully decorating Dot's white apron.

"Mother's coming! " cried Meg, rushing into the kitchen with her flowers. Then she stopped. "Dot Blossom, look what you're done! " she wailed.

Well, there was not much use in scolding, after it was done, and Daddy and Mother Blossom said that since the twins had been so good about helping to get lunch, that they should not be punished beyond having to go without any jelly for that meal.

Of course the four little Blossoms had a great deal to tell about the children they had helped Captain Jenks to rescue from Kidd's Island. Daddy and Mother Blossom had seen the captain in Greenpier and already knew of the rescue, but did not know many of the details that the children now gave them.

"We saw Mr. Harley, " said Mother Blossom, bringing out her darning basket after lunch to one of the pretty trees where the family were fond of sitting.

"I wish he could find Mrs. Harley, " grieved Meg. "Yesterday, when we were playing at Mr. Harley's house, we found a little hobby horse, that must have belonged to one of the boys. I s'pose there wasn't room for it in the trunk. "

"I don't think poor Mrs. Harley packed a trunk, " sighed Mother Blossom. "Mr. Harley says he believes she walked out of the house and took nothing with her except the clothes she wore. She had a suitcase of things for the children, Polly said, and that was all. "

"Well, if that's the case, it's funny we can't find a clue, " remarked Daddy Blossom. "I've looked, and I know Dick has looked, everywhere for some kind of note or even a letter she might have left. There isn't a scrap to build on. "

A few days after this Daddy Blossom announced that he was going to Greenpier on important business.

"I know, Daddy, " shouted Twaddles. "Fireworks for the Fourth of July. "

Father Blossom was going over on the morning boat to do his shopping, and soon after he had gone down to the wharf the four little Blossoms decided to go to "Mr. Harley's house" to play. Mother Blossom, who was writing a long letter to Aunt Polly, was willing, and the four trotted off down the little path their own feet had worn.

"Let's go another way, " suggested Meg suddenly. "We've always said we'd go through the woods, and we always come this same old way. Come on, Bobby, we can't get lost. "

The "woods" that Meg spoke of were mostly underbrush and second growth of trees, with here and there a fine old oak that had escaped the wood-chopper's ax. The children scrambled through the bushes, climbed over the big gray rocks that stood half hidden under a covering of dead leaves and creeping vines, and finally came out behind the Harley shack.

"I never saw this side of it, did you, Meg? " asked Bobby. "Look, this must have been the lean-to where Mrs. Harley did the washing. Yes, here's an old wooden tub all fallen to pieces. "

The children poked about in the rubbish carelessly until Twaddles happened to spy one of the apple trees on the point.

"They're ripe! " he cried in great excitement, though he had had his breakfast less than an hour before. "The apples are ripe, Dot! Mr. Harley said we could eat 'em! "

He and Dot raced for the tree, while Meg followed more slowly. Bobby remained to turn more stones over with his foot.

Presently the others heard him shout.

"Meg! Oh, Meg! Hurry up and see what I've found! "

CHAPTER XV

BOBBY'S GREAT DISCOVERY

Meg ran back, and the twins tumbled pell-mell after her.

"What is it? " they all cried breathlessly. "What is it? "

Bobby held up two small silver mugs.

"Found them down between these two rocks, " he explained. "They must belong to Mr. Harley's little boys. And that isn't all—look here!"

Bobby was so excited his hands shook. He spread three or four stained sheets of paper on the ground.

"It looks like a letter, " said Meg, puzzled.

"It is, " announced Bobby triumphantly. "I can't read it very well, 'cause the writing goes together, but see here's the beginning: 'My dearest Lou, '—that must be Mrs. Harley. "

"Show us where you found 'em, " demanded the twins. "Right down in those little rocks? "

"It's a kind of cave, " said Bobby. "See, in between there's a hollow place and I was just going to see how far it went. It's lined with bricks in there. "

"My d-e-a-r-e-s-t L-o-u, " spelled Meg, who could not read as well as Bobby. "Oh, Bobby, hurry and let Mother read it. Maybe it will say where Mrs. Harley went. "

No going through the woods this time. The four little Blossoms ran as hard as they could, making every possible short cut and paying no attention to inquisitive bushes that reached out brier fingers and tore their clothes. Meg carried the cups and Bobby the letter, and when they reached the bungalow they were all so breathless that at first they could not speak.

"Oh, Mother! " gasped Bobby, when he could speak, "we found a letter to Mrs. Harley. At least we think it is to Mrs. Harley. Back of some rocks. You read it. "

"Does it say where she went? " cried Dot, dancing up and down impatiently. "Does it say where she went, Mother? "

Mother Blossom had to laugh.

"Every one of you sit down and wait until I see what this is Bobby has found, " she commanded. "You are all so excited, I can not half understand what you are trying to tell me. Did you find the cups, too? "

Bobby nodded.

Mother Blossom took the sheets of paper and the children waited as patiently as they could while she read them. When she put them down her eyes were shining.

"This is wonderful! " she exclaimed. "Bobby, my precious, you don't know what you have done. This is not one letter, but three, and written by an uncle and aunt of Mrs. Harley's living in a town called Cordova. It is in Oklahoma. They ask Mrs. Harley to bring the children and come out there to live with them, and I shouldn't be surprised if she had gone there. We must get these letters to Mr. Harley right away. "

"Captain Jenks won't be here till this afternoon and Daddy's coming with him, " said Bobby. "Let me row you over, Mother? "

"I'm afraid you and I will have to go, " answered Mother Blossom. "Chicks, if Daddy were here, you all should go; but I know Meg and the twins will wait patiently for us and we will hurry back and tell you exactly what Mr. Harley says and what he thinks he had better do. "

Meg and Twaddles and Dot wanted to go dreadfully, but they knew that five could not go in one boat and neither Meg nor Bobby could row well enough to manage a boat alone. So the three left behind waited with the best grace they could until Mother Blossom and Bobby came back. They brought Father Blossom and the fireworks with them.

"Did you see Mr. Harley? " was Meg's first question. "Was he glad? Is he going to Oklahoma? "

"Let me fasten the boat, " pleaded Father Blossom. "If our boats drift away some fine night we would be in a pretty fix. Yes, Daughter, we saw Mr. Harley and gave him the letters. He has telegraphed to Cordova, and as soon as he receives a reply he has promised to come over and let us know. "

"How long does it take to telegraph to Cordova? " Twaddles wanted to know.

Father Blossom laughed as he gathered up his packages of fireworks.

"I knew that would be the next question, " he said. "Why, Son, it takes several hours; it may be night, it may be to-morrow morning, before we hear from Mr. Harley. "

"Did the mugs belong to his little boys? " asked Dot, skipping beside her father on the way to the bungalow. "Was he glad to get 'em, Daddy? "

"Very glad, " answered Father Blossom. "The little silver mugs were given to the children by the Greenpier minister when they were christened. "

Throughout the afternoon the children talked of little else than the Harley family. Mr. Harley had asked Father Blossom to search the brick-lined hole between the two rocks, thinking perhaps there might be something else hidden there. He himself was unwilling to leave Greenpier until an answer to his telegram had been received, even though he knew it could not come very soon.

Father Blossom searched carefully, but there was nothing else in the hole.

Mr. Harley did not come that afternoon, but the next morning the Blossoms had just finished breakfast when he knocked at the door.

But such a changed Mr. Harley!

His eyes were bright and clear, and his face was beaming with happiness. He wore a new suit of clothes and a new hat and was freshly shaved. The Blossoms knew instantly that he had had good news.

"Everything is all right, " he announced in a ringing voice. "Had an answer from Cordova at nine o'clock last night. Lou and the boys are living with her Uncle Matthew, and they want me to come out there as quick as trains will carry me. I'm off this morning! "

"I'm so glad, " Mother Blossom kept saying. "I'm so glad. "

"Can't be half as glad as I am, " answered the smiling Mr. Harley. "And to think if it hadn't been for this boy here I never would have found them! I'll never forget the Blossoms if I live to be a hundred. "

Mr. Harley, we'll tell you here, did find his wife and two sons in Oklahoma, and as they did not want to return to Apple Tree Island where they had been so unhappy, he settled down in Cordova with them and helped the uncle to farm. Uncle Matthew Dexter and Aunt Sue were both growing old and they were very glad to have a younger and stronger man to lend them a hand. As for the two boys and Mrs. Harley, they declared that they never would give them up, so it was fortunate that Mr. Harley liked to farm. Dick and Herbert grew into fine young lads. So we may leave the Harley family with a comfortable mind.

Fourth of July dawned hot and sunny on Apple Tree Island. Captain Jenks came over in his motor-boat and brought a huge chunk of ice for the freezing of the ice-cream. He had been invited to stay to dinner and to see the fireworks in the evening, and when, after dinner, it grew so hot that Father Blossom declared the sun would certainly set fire to the sparklers without any punk, the jolly captain loaded "all hands" on board The Sarah and took them off for a sail around the island.

There was plenty of breeze then, you may be sure, and the children had great fun lighting their sparklers and hanging them over the rail to burn. They had to keep away from the engine with their "fizzers, " as the captain would call them, because he said he wouldn't trust even guaranteed fireworks to be harmless around a gasoline engine, but they had plenty of excitement without blowing up the good ship Sarah.

"Why, we're not going home—we're going to Greenpier! " cried Meg, when they had sailed around the island and were headed for the opposite shore.

Mother and Father Blossom looked very mysterious, but said nothing, and Captain Jenks answered all questions by ordering them not to talk to "the man at the wheel. "

When The Sarah bumped into the Greenpier wharf, the four little Blossoms made a simultaneous discovery.

"Jud! " they shrieked in unison. "Jud Apgar! Oh, Juddy! "

It was Jud, Jud grinning happily with a traveling bag in one hand and a box in the other.

"Go easy now, " he warned the children as they descended upon him in a body. "Miss Polly sent your mother some fresh eggs—you don't want to smash 'em, do you? "

Mother Blossom rescued the egg box, and the children escorted Jud on deck and introduced him to Captain Jenks.

"Guess you surprised some folks, " said the captain, shaking Jud's hand as though he were very glad to see him. "Some folks couldn't see why we should come to Greenpier on a Wednesday afternoon and a holiday at that. "

Mother and Father Blossom and Aunt Polly had planned the surprise, it seemed. Jud could never leave Brookside Farm for long at one time in the Summer, there was so much work to be done, but Aunt Polly assured him that he could easily be spared for a few days' visit to Apple Tree Island. She had planned it with Father and Mother Blossom through letters and they had kept the secret successfully.

If the afternoon was still hot when they reached home, no one knew it. The whole island had to be shown to Jud, and he had to see the Harley shack and hear of the discovery of the silver mugs and the letters. It was supper time before the children realized it and then, in a little while, it was dark.

"Dark enough for fireworks? " said Twaddles for the twentieth time, and he bounced with delight when Father Blossom said:

"Dark enough to begin, I think. "

Mother Blossom and the children and Captain Jenks sat on the steps of the bungalow while Father Blossom and Jud set off the fireworks. Each child was allowed to apply the punk to one piece, but they soon found it was better fun to sit quietly and watch.

"There goes a flower-pot! " cried Meg, as a brilliant shower of red and yellow sparks bloomed out against the velvet blackness of the Summer night.

"One, two, three, four, five, six, seven—seven stars, " counted Bobby as Jud set off a Roman candle.

"Now a rocket! " said Mother Blossom, and Captain Jenks gave a hurrah as the beautiful shooting star thing hissed and fell far out into Sunset Lake.

Father Blossom and Jud were kept busy setting off the many pieces, for Jud had brought more in his bag, and when they lit the last red light it was discovered that Dot was fast asleep sitting upright against a porch post.

It was a tired and sleepy family that, Jud carrying Dot, marched to bed when the red light had burned itself out. But they were immensely happy. So was Captain Jenks, whistling on his way to his boat—nothing would induce him to stay all night. So was the Harley family far out in Oklahoma. And they were all happy for the same reason.

THE END